FOREVER CURIOUS

JETSE DE VRIES

Forever Curious is a work of fiction. Names, characters, business, events and incidents are the products of the author's imagination. Any resemblance to actual persons, living or dead, or actual events is purely coincidental.

Future Uplift Books

Jetse de Vries
's-Hertogenbosch
The Netherlands

ISBN: 978-90-831639-0-1

Cover art "City Ship" by Maciej Rebisz

9 789083 163901

CONTENTS

INTRO: INTO THE PIT

Na-Yeli Maya approaches the alien object with a mix of pride, trepidation, and curiosity. Unsure of her exact role–champion? explorer? scientist?–she's well aware that she may be the next in a long line of adventurers that went in, but never came out.

An impenetrable, perfectly black sphere–only blocked-out starlight, a fast-rotating magnetic field, and a massively complex gravitational footprint betray its presence–with two opposite holes, dubbed the Enigmatic Object. Its radius is approximately 86 kilometers, or exactly 2^{132} Planck Lengths, as one brilliant mind deduced. One hole is blocked with–what seems to be–a spherically shaped, highly charged piece of strange matter. For reference's sake, it's called the South Pole. The other one–the North Pole–is not covered, and nicknamed 'the shutter'. The rest of the sphere–the outer shell–is an invisible, impenetrable barrier that reduces any normal matter touching it to its atomic constituents–a process named 'spaghettification' as the molecules are strung out until they break–and has proven impervious to exotic matter like neutronium, quark matter and strangelet, as well.

Most of the time, through a cycle so complex it verges on the chaotic, the North Pole is closed. At unpredictable times, it will open in a truly minuscule manner–micrometers, possibly even nanometers–and then be fully opaque, again. Only once every two-hundred-and-thirty-three human days–or exactly 2^{168} Planck Times, as calculated by the same brilliant mind–it opens, bang on schedule, wide enough to let an object with a diameter of one meter through.

Its widest opening remains for just over two seconds. Barely enough to let one vessel out, and another vessel in. Through carefully negotiated treaties–after a number of intense interstellar wars over access to the Enigmatic Object decimated several galactic civilizations–each alien species gets a turn and is only allowed to go in during the second second, in order to let someone–whoever it is–out first. Timing is everything. Timing is sacrosanct. Timing is make or break.

Not only is the window of entry short, but the tidal forces surrounding it formidable. Anything with more than one hundred kilograms of mass, or bigger than one meter across will be irresistibly drawn towards the ominous outer shell and 'spaghettified' into its atomic constituents.

Na-Yeli is dropped from her mothership and the spherical pod (with an exoskin of metamaterials that can both transform and shape-shift) in which she will explore the unknown object—while its one hundred-and-seventy-two kilometer diameter makes it cosmically small, inside it is said to contain whole worlds in miniature—is weighed and manufactured to the picogram and picometer. Her aim must be true and her timing must be right: one nanometer off, or one millisecond late, and she's toast. Or more accurately, spaghetti on toast.

Using the lasers of the mothership for course corrections—so she can enter the black enigma with the maximum possible amount of life support and equipment—she aims at the opening, dead center, in a perfectly perpendicular approach. Maximum acceleration at full laser power, so her passage time is as short as possible. Her pod heating up just short of cooking her—this has been rehearsed to exhaustion, and dog knows she might need the extra energy—she races to the forbidding gate, wondering if other explorers were cutting it as fine as she is. A mental brace, a sharp gravitational tug from all directions at once, and ... she's in.

SPIRAL DOGFIGHTS

Resistance is the first thing she experiences, as something is slowing down the pod that is also her extended exoskeleton, made of metamaterials. Noise immediately follows, does it have an atmosphere? While her sensors take samples for the spectrometers, the shape-shifting metamaterials of her exoskin quickly transform her sphere into something much more aerodynamic. Stretching from her fetus-like curl into a diver's posture with arms out wide to accommodate the miniature airplane her pod's become, her wings stretched very wide to provide sufficient lift, she keeps heading straight down, trying to maintain her speed.

Helium, pure helium, her equipment reads, with an atmospheric pressure of zero point three bar. At a frigid one hundred Kelvin, her hull's metamaterials have switched to maximum insulation to preserve her heat reserves. It's almost pitch dark and in order to avoid running into something she has to keep radar, lidar, and sonar running at full resolution. Until her sensors have finished their complete run of the spectrum. Thank dog, nearly uniform background radiation deep in the ultraviolet. Her light sensors adapt and there is a dim kind of visibility. Only two hundred meters deep and rather faint, but it'll have to do. Anything better than true darkness, as there's not even starlight in here.

She keeps heading straight at the center, which at this speed she should reach within half an hour. Unfortunately, but not unexpectedly, it's not that easy. Within a few minutes both her sonar, lidar and radar detect a hard reflection, spherical in shape. A quick extrapolation reveals a sphere with a one-hundred-and-forty-four-point-five kilometer diameter. They're in an outer layer between two shells.

It confirms the extremely classified information her people managed to extract–at great expense– from some of the known alien races. This ominous sphere has shells within its outer, impenetrable shell, and–hopefully accessible–layers within these shells. If the inter-shell spacing is regular, there should be seven equidistant shells each approximately twelve point three kilometers apart, with the inner one—let's call it the Core—a sphere with a twenty-four-point-six kilometer diameter. Thus six layers—including from this one, content unknown—of twelve point three kilometers thick before one gets to the Core. *If* the spacing is indeed regular.

However, she just measured that this dark Helium layer is thirteen-point-seventy-five kilometers thick, which throws the equidistant idea out of the window. It probably won't be the first surprise the Enigmatic Object throws at her.

The surface straight below isn't a perfect sphere, though. There is a little ridge with a different reflection signature. It matches the characteristics of the strange matter 'stopper' at the South Pole of the outermost shell to a T, signifying that the opening of the second outermost shell will be at its opposite end—the South Pole—the long way around. This seems to confirm the alien info stating that the openings are at opposite ends: enter through the North Pole, exit through the South Pole, enter through the South Pole, exit through the North Pole, etcetera. The shortest way follows a longitude, unless the builders of this Enigmatic Object are playing a prank, and put the opening at a random spot.

The analytical half of Na-Yeli's brain doesn't think so. This construct is too—well, if not regular than–logical for the opening not to be at the other, hopefully, non-stopped end. The personality beneath the right-side artistic hemisphere of her brain agrees. Now, which longitude? There are a near-infinite number of them, all the shortest way. In her computer implant–connecting her with the triple-redundant quantum computer distributed through the innermost layer of her exoskin–she throws a quantum dice and chooses one at random.

While there is a gravitational pull to the center, this layer–throughout its thirteen point seventy-five kilometers thickness between its two impenetrable shells–is not uniform in pressure and temperature. There are thermals that Na-Yeli tries to ride as much as possible because she never knows when she will really need her energy reserves. Since the gravitational pull measured by her instruments is only one-twentieth of Earth's, even the faintest of updrafts can lift her, minimizing her energy expenditure. In the polar region, things appear to be quiet, and Na-Yeli seems to be the only intelligent, or even sentient, agent around. In order to save energy, Na-Yeli switches off her sonar and lidar and continues onwards, trusting her radar and line-of-sight in the dim ultraviolet.

The tranquility doesn't last. When she crosses the 66th parallel, she has her first encounter. Rising above the globular horizon, an unknown number of UFOs are approaching. Barely big enough to register on her radar, too small to be counted quickly. A flock of ET birds? An alien swarm of autonomous machines? While their trajectory seems to be matching hers, it doesn't feel interceptive. Thrusters and weapons at the ready, Na-Yeli waits, while telling her communication AI to transmit–what she hopes are–peaceful messages at select wavelengths. In the meantime, she sticks to her longitudinal route.

In the dim, ultraviolet reflection, there is a metallic sheen to the extraterrestrial flock, whose double rotors give them an insect-like appearance. *Well, botswarm,* Na-Yeli inadvertently calls them, *do your worst.* They match her course, then perform a few circles around her, the only exchange mutual observations. After which they seem to lose interest and head back to where they came from.

"Did you get any response?" She asks the communication AI.

–none whatsoever– it signals *–boring–*

The communication AI–and its two redundant copies–exist in a sentient mode as vague and unknown as the neural networks it's based upon.

That is, it has a kind of awareness–maybe even a rudimentary consciousness–but nobody knows exactly how it works. In practice, it churns with relish through alien algorithms, unutterable languages, and obscure grammar, but won't touch emotion with a ten-foot pole. As such, it appears stand-offish and curt, but Na-Yeli doesn't mind, as she has more than enough on her plate, already, such as the first life forms she encounters within the Enigmatic Object.

A quick peek-a-boo, Na-Yeli thinks, *or a heads-up for the* real *welcoming committee?* Apart from being deeply mysterious, the situation is also highly complex. Humanity is a Johnny-come-lately on the interstellar stage, and no one knows exactly how many previous alien races have accessed this ominous object. Let alone how many of these previous explorers have perished, returned, gone native, or have transformed in some way. Not to mention which–if any–of the ecosystems inside the Universe's biggest mystery were native, to begin with.

We may be biting off way more than we can chew, Na-Yeli thinks, *but damn us if we're not going to try, anyway.*

She continues her trek in eerie silence.

With its entrance/exit holes alternately at the North and South Poles, the alien edifice–humanity refers to it as 'the Enigmatic Object'—not only has a strong electromagnetic field, but this field rotates very fast, as well. This field—widely known, as it is measurable outside it—is used by its explorers for harvesting energy, which is used to recharge their batteries. This recharging effect increases the closer an explorer is to the 'equator'—the rotational plane or the plane of the ecliptic. Using this eliminates the need of bringing one's own power supply—if one's willing to take the chance—and the precious weight limit can be used for other equipment. Or weapons.

Quite suddenly, another flock of aliens is appearing—if the first flock appeared at a latitude that would, roughly speaking, equate with the polar circle on Earth, then these show up close to the Tropic of Cancer—who look quite a bit bigger, and more numerous than the first one. Her radar only picked them up at the last moment, suggesting they're either impervious to radar, or have evolved stealth properties. They're not unlike bats—mouse-like bodies with huge wings. Again, Na-Yeli tells the communication AI to try to make contact.

Their trajectory is very straightforward, they keep going right at her, with no sign of changing course. That's crazy, do they want to smother her or suchlike? It does seem so, as their positioning becomes ever tighter so that the wings of the alien bats in front overlap those of the rows behind them, effectively creating a living, flying wall closing in on her. An alien bat-wall, of all things, a flying bat-mat.

"Any reaction?" Na-Yeli queries the communication AI.

–nothing I can discern– the communication AI signals (its words are projected at the bottom of Na-Yeli's point-of-view, synchronized with its drone-like vocalization, reminding Na-Yeli it's a weak AI rather than an actual human) *–just a cacophony of high-frequency screeches that are barely discernible from chaos. probably mindless shrieks from a frantic flock–*

They don't react to any of her transmissions, neither do a few, carefully aimed light bombs hamper their advance in any way. If anything, the huge flashes of light seem to accelerate their approach. Na-Yeli starts an evading maneuver, trying to pass them on the right only to see that five more of these bat-mats are closing in on her from the top, bottom, left, right, and behind.

She was concentrating so much on the very first one approaching her so much that she completely overlooked the other ones. No room for a quick 180-degree turnaround, she's almost surrounded. In subconscious strata, one of her personalities is cursing her over-analytic mind for providing too many distractions. Yet, the situation is not dire enough for it to rise to the fore.

Na-Yeli is committed to the right, and a squeeze-through between the forward and right bat-mat looks increasingly unlikely as they close formation. A barrage of light bombs. Unfortunately, these don't seem to faze them. And the bat-mats keep closing in.

Na-Yeli's run out of friendly options. With extreme reluctance, she fires two small torpedoes at the alien bats blocking her way. Both torpedoes hit their target almost dead center, and explode. The shockwaves rip the wings of the bats apart, and they fall, breaking the formation. Na-Yeli's wings quickly swing backward as she and her craft squeeze through the opening they created.

Out of the trap, wings back in the optimum lift position, Na-Yeli takes a long, swooping curve to see if the six bat-mats are regrouping. To her bafflement, they do nothing of the kind but are diving after the alien bats she hit. With their wings in tatters, they spiral downwards in the light gravity towards the invisible yet foreboding shell below.

Are the rest trying to save their wounded kinsfolk? *Or am I thinking too anthropocentric?* Na-Yeli wonders. The previously highly-ordered bat-mats have broken their tight formation, and are now one big, chaotic swarm chasing their falling kin. Yet none of the healthy ones try to overtake their injured companions. They follow but keep a certain distance.

The torpedo-struck aliens–Na-Yeli can only hope that they've died, already–spiral down towards the invisible barrier. Flashes of light, almost blinding in this near-total dimness, follow–seconds later–by thin, metallic crackles that represent thunder in a cold, helium-gas environment as the remnants of the falling alien bats are spaghettified–their skin, flesh, and bones ripped apart by intense, singular forces–to their atomic constituents.

A feeding frenzy follows.

The alien bat swarm dives as close as they dare–while fighting for pole position–in order to harvest as much of the liberated atoms and energy as possible. *It makes sense*, Na-Yeli thinks, *food has to come from somewhere*. And there's no reason why cannibalism should not develop in aliens, especially in an environment as cold and forbidding as this.

Then, realization strikes: *I was meant to be that meal*. She and her craft are much bigger than the average alien bat, and by smothering her in flight, they probably hoped she would be the one falling to her doom, and end up as their spaghettified snack.

Both the spaghettifying–she didn't realize that so much energy and light would be released by the

17

process—and the feeding frenzy of the bat swarms are a sight to behold. It becomes so vehement that she wouldn't be surprised if a few other alien bats are—partially or totally—spaghettified in the fray. The atoms of the helium atmosphere don't seem to spaghettify, though. They're already loose atoms—no chemical bonds—and while they will get squeezed, they probably remain intact and then just bounce off.

She gets off with a warning, a stern one, at that. On a related note, she now thanks the foresight of her scientific team who brought up the idea of a dynamic-positioning balloon. When she's resting or sleeping, she needs to stay atop the underlying shell and can turn part of her shape-shifting, metamaterial exoskeleton in a small vacuum balloon, keeping her aloft. *I suppose all creatures in this helium layer will have found a way to 'hover' when resting,* she thinks, *talk about survival pressure.*

Things remain quiet for a while as Na-Yeli makes good progress. By Earth reckoning, she's about to cross the Tropic of Cancer. A blip appears on her radar, further south, heading in a westerly direction. *Almost slant to my course,* Na-Yeli thinks, *let's see if it keeps that heading.*

As Na-Yeli comes closer, it does indeed. In the meantime, the blip grows into a blimp and further enlarges into a dirigible. Airships make so much sense in this environment, that Na-Yeli's quite surprised to see the first one only now.

At this point, Na-Yeli must be within the dirigible's radar range. Yet the dirigible shows no signs of seeing her, not accelerating nor slowing down, and keeping its heading. Na-Yeli is torn: should she ignore it and keep going south, or hail it and risk hostilities?

On the one hand, she has a mission. But that mission is pretty broadly defined, and 'exploration' features quite high in her mission statement. On the other hand, she can't quite believe that every stranger she meets in here has to be hostile. That would make as much sense as expecting that each and every alien in here will treat her as an honored guest. Some will be hostile, some won't. On top of that, it's quite empty in here, and she wants to make the most of each encounter.

She's made up her mind—she can resist everything except temptation, and mysteries are her greatest temptations—and heads for the dirigible. Neither does she want to surprise them, so she's sending messages its way across a range of electromagnetic frequencies, sonar sound pulses, and lidar flashes. No reaction at all from the mysterious dirigible as she comes closer and closer.

She's within ten meters of the–relatively large–airship and still no beep from the silent blimp. A rectangular bridge hangs on the bottom of the cigar-shaped airship. Its windows are dark. Na-Yeli flies as close to those windows as she can, but they only show her reflection. The dirigible seems abandoned and–for all purposes–dead.

Still, she's got to know and makes an improvised hook that she can easily hang around one of the ropes that tie the bridge to the airship's body. Once she's tested if the connection is true, she retracts–transforms them into something more manageable –her wings, then hauls herself towards the door of the bridge. To her utter surprise, the door is not locked.

No gasses escape, nor are sucked in as she carefully opens the door, meaning the pressure in the bridge cabin is equal to that of this layer's atmosphere. She goes in to find an unmanned bridge. She checks all other cabins but finds no signs of life. She hangs up a few makeshift floodlights and sets them to a low brightness as not to disturb her night vision. Then she recognizes the symbols on the bridge.

Swing Monkees, one of the most human-like aliens in this galaxy. Simian bodies with large brainpans. Their innate tendency to hang in the huge trees of their low gravity planet made them a natural fit for space travel, once the shielding problem was solved. If anything, Na-Yeli'd expect them to be much farther into the Enigmatic Object. Yet no signs of actual Swing Monkees in this ghost ship.

It's a shame, as humanity and the Swing Monkees get along quite well, and she would have loved to exchange info and experiences. But in this dirigible, nobody's home, except for a message, written with a red liquid, on the wall in front of her. It's repeated—now that she knows where to look for —in other places on the walls, ceiling, and floor, albeit the same message with different phrasing. Roughly translated—she doesn't even need the communication AI for that—they read:

"Don't go South, for there is The Squad."

"Those who try to cross The Squad will surely perish."

"Abandon all hope, all ye who meet The Squad."

Similar messages across the bridge and the crew cabins. The dirigible is abandoned, even if her air-powered autopilot is still working, stuck at maintaining a westerly heading, circling this layer for dog knows how long (she almost thought 'for all eternity', but that would be a bit too dramatic). No weapons or other equipment on board, so after a final check, Na-Yeli leaves the ghost ship, empty-handed.

She can't quite put her finger on it, but it reminds her of something. Cherishing the enigma, she decides not to check similar cases in her database.

She's been going for about two hours, or about forty-five kilometers now, by dead reckoning (including the time she lost during the exchange with the bat-walls) and is approaching the south subtropical region.

In this energy-rich area—assuming the local fauna has adaptations that leverage the fast-rotating magnetic field—there seems to be more action. There are not just more bat-walls—which she's now learned to discern from a great distance—but other flying creatures, as well. Some that are attacked by the bat-walls, some that seem to attack these flying mats: predators?

Her radar is showing a small echo in the distance. Which is interesting, as the bat-walls are invisible to her radar, so she needs her sonar and lidar—each with their own limitations—to pick them up over a longer distance (essential in this environment with limited visibility). Something that conducts electromagnetic radiation. Possibly an artificial construct?

It's approaching fast at a gliding speed that triggers her envy. Or is it powered? Closer up, she notices it's not one single UFO, but four, flying in tight formation. She's on a long glide down from a nice thermal a few minutes back, so they're coming at her from above. Very fast.

She makes an evasive maneuver, feinting to the left, then diving to the right. Three of the four alien avians miss her, but the most right of them manages to nick her on her left wing with its nose. It's sharp enough to scratch the shape-shifting metamaterials of her hull. Do they want to spear her?

As she is now above them, she can have a quick, line-of-sight look. She has no idea how long she will be in here, and while her battery health reads just over eighty percent, she tries to travel as energy-efficient as possible. Therefore, she keeps the mini-cameras that are spread all over her hull behind a protective layer, relying on the trio of radar, lidar, and sonar in this limited sight layer. The disadvantage being that she only has a vague impression of incoming aliens at first.

But now her 'eyes'–forward-looking cameras with quick-opening caps that are positioned in line with her real eyes–can take a few quick snapshots, helped by a synchronized flash. The extraterrestrial avians have X-shaped wings and long, thin, sharp– she can acknowledge– snouts.

Their 'wings'–for lack of a better word–are not quite the flexible, often fractal-shaped, streamlined versions of terrestrial avians. They seem much more rigidly geometric as if not gliding aerodynamics but something else is powering their flight. Yet Na-Yeli can't discern any powered mode of propulsion on them, no propellers, nor jets or thrusters of any kind.

Their 'X-wing' shape doesn't seem to make much sense aerodynamically speaking. Usually, one needs two big, horizontal wings for lift, and one needs only small vertical ones for steering, any bigger and the vertical 'wings' will cause unnecessary drag. Nevertheless, on these X-kites– as she silently baptizes them–the wings are all exactly the same size. So either their vertical wings are too small, or their horizontal ones too big.

As if to banish any doubts about their maneuverability, here they come again, making a few turns much sharper than Na-Yeli thought possible. Much sharper than she can perform, unaided by propulsion. Approaching even faster than on their first run, Na-Yeli can't use the same dodging movement. Coming in from two sides at once, a sandwich attack she can only evade by making an even sharper turn. Reluctantly, she switches on her ion thruster and escapes just in the nick of time.

Or maybe not, as a second X-kite manages to leave a nick in her right wing, this time. Na-Yeli doesn't want to fight back, not particularly to avoid starting a war–'what happens in the Enigmatic Object (EO) stays in the EO' is part of the treaty–but because it's not what she's here for. She's sent to find out the secrets–if any–of the Enigmatic Object. Each alien race has a special name for the neigh-impenetrable dark, globular construct; and nobody has been able to extract its deepest secrets. She just wants to get at the heart of it, both literally and figuratively, and these X-kites with their hounding dogfights are–in her viewpoint–merely an obstacle. She prefers to pass or circumvent obstacles, not destroy them. In general–as with the bat-mats–she tries to avoid confrontations, which are time- and energy-consuming, as much as possible. Nevertheless, she has weapons.

Two strategies cross her mind. Either she fights back, wasting precious energy, time, and effort. Or she avoids them one more time, and then makes a run for the South Pole, hoping–assuming–that there will be an opening–not a shutter–there. For the latter, she has to be sure that she's faster than the X-kites pursuing her. And that they won't follow her into the next layer. Talk about the devil and the deep dark sea.

As they approach her for the third time, she arranges her feints in such a manner that her final escape leads her south. These X-kites are swift, but through her ion thruster and her shape-shifting hull, she is swifter. Seemingly by the skin of her teeth, she evades them. In reality, though, this time none of them came close enough to nick her.

Then she feels a sharp pain in both her wings– where her arms are–accompanied by a flash of lightning near her tail. *What the hell*, she thinks, ignoring the pain, *they throw lightning bolts?* Her instruments acknowledge her suspicions, she's been hit by a massive discharge of static electricity.

She thanks the foresight of her battle planners, who drilled her to put up her Faraday cage before a fight, just in case. Normally, Na-Yeli uses advanced rectenna elements for recharging her batteries by tapping energy from the Enigmatic Object's fast-rotating electromagnetic field. But this will not work when her Faraday cage is up, and switching between the two modes takes some time. Luckily, she got the Faraday cage up just in time.

Thus, the metamaterials of her exoskin act like a Faraday cage and protect her. But the two nicks that the X-Kites managed to get on her wings allow some static discharge to go in. Her instruments survived, and she's a little worse for wear, but she can't take hits like this indefinitely.

Nevertheless, this might explain the X-Kites' superb maneuverability. Somehow they tap into the fast-rotating electromagnetic field of this layer. Their wings could be of an electromagnetically permeable material ... Take it a step further: an electromagnetically permeable material that can both be used as generator and motor ... Two of their X-wings can absorb power from the rapidly rotating electromagnetic field, power that then can be used to generate a perpendicular field in the other two wings ... And as such provide magnetic counter-forces enabling its surprising maneuverability ...

It's crazy, but the best explanation she can come up with. Now don't use precious time wondering how such strange creatures could evolve–or were they designed?–but find a way to test this hypothesis. Here they come again. *First these bat-mats out of hell*, she thinks, *and now this. Is it going to be like this all the time?* She's not happy at the prospect. Under her subconscious surface, though, another personage is relishing the challenge. *Bring it on!*

They attack in a diamond formation. A classic, Na-Yeli realizes, in whatever direction she tries to flee, at least one will follow. They must have noticed that's she vulnerable to their static electricity charges and hope that one of them can get a full, direct hit. Na-Yeli's been trained for this, exhaustively to say the least, but this part of her brain is not optimally suited for extended dogfights. She remembers attack and defense tactics, has lightning-quick access to all human-known dogfights in history through her computer implants, but these hinder her more than help her, as she's spoiled for choice and can't make up her mind. *A few more minutes,* she thinks, *and the self-repairing properties of my exoskin's metamaterials have fixed the holes. I'll be impervious to their lightning bolts.*

She feints, counter-feints and triple-feints as the four X-Kites are closing in. Then she gives her ion thruster full throttle and heads straight through the center of the diamond formation. This takes three of her four adversaries by surprise, yet one reacts incredibly fast by jabbing her with the sharp end of its snout. She feels something breaking–a quick check on her vital signs tells her it must be the tip of the X-Kite's snout–but the same vital signs show that her exoskin has a long rip of almost fifty centimeters long. *So much for fast repairs,* she thinks.

In the next encounter, Na-Yeli reacts too slow and two X-Kites hit her with their static electricity bolts. Entering through the big rip, it trips the intelligent fuses of half her sensors and hurts her human body like hell. So much, she has trouble staying conscious. *Oh shit, I can't fail this early into my–* and she faints after she feels someone else is taking over.

If her adversaries could see Na-Yeli's face, they might have noticed the subtle changes in her expression. The open, curious yet calculating gaze is replaced by a grim set of her jaw and the aggressive twitching of her eyes, always looking for enemies. KillBitch is in command, and she glowers with hate. She hates the pain that's tearing through her body–even as it feeds her hate–she hates this mess of a battle situation she's saddled up with, and she hates, hates her opponents who inflicted all this damage. But, most of all, she hates to lose.

She doesn't have much time to gather her thoughts. Half her system is down, still recovering. Only the afterburner of her ion thruster is still functional, and while the small nicks have healed on her exoskin, it will be at least half an hour before the big rip is patched. However, she still has most of her lethal weapons.

The X-Kites come in for the kill. They know she's taken two big hits and might think her maneuverability is limited, and they'd be right. KillBitch strengthens the impression by intentionally putting a wobble in her glide. *Pretend I'm almost down*, she doesn't even think this, as it's a survival trait at least as old as humanity itself.

They come in from two directions, above and below. *The top ones to shoot me down*, her battle instinct recognizes, *the bottom ones to finish the job.* From both previous encounters, confirmed by a quick calculation of her computer implants, she knows exactly when she will be in the X-Kites lightning bolt firing range. A split second before that, she transforms from her flight posture into an almost perfectly spherical fetus curl, the shape-shifting metamaterials barely keeping up with her, also ensuring her ion thruster is pointed up.

Undeterred by her strange maneuver, the top two X-Kites fire at her, at will. She's hit, not once, not twice, but several times. However, KillBitch has curled up in such a manner that the big rip in her hull armature is inside. Subsequently, only a small trickle gets through. *It tickles*, her battle-hardened soul scoffs, *is that all you've got?* In the meantime, she falls, her fall accelerated by short bursts from the ion thruster's afterburner.

She drops below the two lower X-Kites that, for good measure, also shower her with a volley of hits. Then they follow her to the fatal barrier below, preparing to feast on her sputtering remains. *They're coming in closer and closer*, KillBitch's battle instinct observes, *must be thinking I'm dead meat already*.

Her sonar and radar still work perfectly, enabling KillBitch to estimate the distance to the skin of spaghettification very precisely. At the last possible moment, she uncurls from her spherical fetus position into a long rocket with only tail fins and ignites her afterburner at full power. She misses the deadly barrier by millimeters and is up and above the four X-Kites before these have had a chance to reverse. She readies four of her mini-torpedoes, aims, and fires, expertly hitting all four X-Kites without a second thought.

Then KillBitch reverts to a more fuel-efficient flying shape, and heads for the South Pole, while her backward-aimed cameras carefully monitor the plummeting remains of her opponents, ready to go back if necessary. But she doesn't need to, all four X-Kites plunge to an explosive, angel-hair-pasta stairway to heaven. KillBitch isn't interested. *Let the scavengers have 'em*, is the last thought of KillBitch's warrior soul as the Slow CEO returns to the fore.

E ventually, humanity–like all alien races that achieved a certain level of technological development–heard the siren song. Gravity waves in such a pattern that they had to be artificial. The pattern was as straightforward as it was irresistible: repetitive binary numbers representing the first eleven primes, the five Planck units, and Universal coordinates of its position over time. *Here I am, come hither*.

A trap, a call for help, or interstellar spam? Whatever it was–or will prove to be–only the most Luddite of souls would deny that it had accelerated the development of interstellar travel. While the speed of light limit still applies to everyone–human or alien, all had their version of Einstein–humanity had to go there. Especially as it was not in our quadrant of the Milky Way.

Inevitably, they found they weren't the only ones, and certainly not the first. Whole alien civilizations had arisen and fallen, epic interstellar wars had been fought, and complex interspecies treaties had been forged on the anvil of the Enigmatic Object.

So alien it made other aliens seem like garden variety critters. So inscrutable it made string theory look like a simplified Rubik's cube. So impenetrable it gave the supermassive black hole at the center of the Milky Way a run for its photons.

Once the regular, if rare, opening sequence of the 'shutter' had been figured out, many had gone in. A few had come out. None had come close to

32

finding out the Enigmatic Object's inner secrets, inner workings, let alone its *raison d'être*.

Despite the treaty, there was a huge black market in classified information that certain alien species claimed they had extracted from the Enigmatic Object. The veracity of that information was as fluent as the momentum of an electron whose position had just been nailed. The speculations about what was in its–supposed– seven layers dwarfed the greatest myths and legends ever created by pre-starfaring cultures.

Nevertheless, the human race had bartered hugely valuable goods to get inside information. After all, what's the worth of highly desirable goods, rare materials, or other earthly matters when the prize was the secret of the Universe?

More skeptic souls proposed that humanity–or any alien race, for that matter–would be better off putting all that effort into finding out the secret of the Universe through the scientific method. The problem with that, time-honored approach, was that it was facing an insurmountable obstacle. Like the way Moore's Law in the early 21st Century and quantum computing in the early 22nd had run into the physical limits of their respective technologies, the scientific method had run into a Planck wall. The energy densities required to truly test the latest version of string theory–or its many competing theories—were unachievable in any practical manner.

No interspecies cooperation was going to pay for an accelerator the size of the Milky Way—never mind if it *could* be built—when every theory agreed that its findings would only be the next intermediate step in the twisted stairway to the ultimate theory of everything. Energy densities of Big Bang proportions were required, and nobody wanted to sacrifice the Universe itself, with all its intelligent species, to find out its secrets, in the extremely unlikely case they could.

The siren song of an Enigmatic Object of a more manageable size was much more appealing than neigh-unending investments in good old experimental physics. So humanity, like many species before them, had prepared one of their best, an explorer-cum-scientist-cum-champion, armed with their best technology and most up-to-date knowledge, to go down the inscrutable, cosmic rabbit hole.

Which is where Na-Yeli Maya finds herself, fighting to stay alive in the very first layer, with no time to find out what's in there, what makes it tick, let alone why it's there in the first place. *Nobody said it would be easy*, she thought, *even worse, nobody guaranteed I would come out alive.* Nevertheless, she's extremely excited to be here.

In the aftermath of the deadly dogfights, Na-Yeli takes stock. Battery health lower than thirty percent, a big rip in her exoskin–which is slowly healing–and forty percent of her sensors offline, also being repaired. The repairs consume materials and the batteries need to be recharged. For the moment, all is clear according to her radar, lidar, and sonar, so she reprograms the metamaterials of her exoskin to become permeable to electromagnetic radiation, and extends two cylindrical fins, doped with conducting materials, perpendicular to the Enigmatic Objects quickly rotating field, in this converting a tiny amount of it into energy for charging her batteries. At some point, she will need to replenish her physical stock of materials, too, if she keeps losing metamaterials from her hull during battles.

Using all the updrafts she can find in this frigid heliumscape, Na-Yeli makes her way to the South Pole using as little energy as possible. Slowly, her batteries charge up to above eighty percent. But the peace and quiet don't last long, as a flock of alien birds is approaching from the Southwest. It makes Na-Yeli wonder if anything ever gets the time to sleep–even in the majority of alien races, the sleep cycle was an ingrained evolutionary tool–without becoming prey. *That's probably why, so far, all of them come in flocks*, she thinks, *so one half can guard the other*. Her computer implants point out that there are beings that let only one hemisphere sleep while the other wakes, but this particular adaptation would not work for Na-Yeli. So she better get out of here before the need for sleep arises.

With a weary sigh, she pulls in her recharging fins, reprograms her exoskin to Faraday cage mode, and mentally prepares for battle. But, even in the far distance, there is something familiar about this flock. A flickering, metallic sheen as from a multitude of double rotors. The cylindrical silhouettes of exactly the same size she remembers –and her instruments confirm. The botswarm she met when she first got in. Is it the same botswarm, or a different one?

The previous one was, if not hostile, at least indifferent. Na-Yeli strongly prefers not to waste a lot of energy and effort with another pointless battle. Yet the last, almost lethal encounter is still fresh in her mind.

She grinds her teeth, brings everything up to battle readiness, and lets the botswarm approach, ready to either fire or flee at the slightest sign of trouble. But exactly like the botswarm at the Arctic regions, this one also matches her course, and flies a few circles around her, never really coming close enough for direct contact. Again, to the utter disappointment of the communication AI, they don't react to any of Na-Yeli's transmissions–as neither the bat-mats and the X-Kites did–only observe. Again, like the first encounter, they seem to lose interest and head back to where they came from, in utter silence.

Na-Yeli travels onwards. According to her instruments–based mainly on the alien object's magnetic field strength–and a combination of gyro headings, distance traveled, and dead reckoning, Na-Yeli estimates that she must be getting close to the South Pole of the second shell. The environment below has, as above, become dim, quiet, and again–thankfully–rather boring. In the distance, a circle of light appears.

Visible light, even. Which is good, since the need to keep radar, lidar, and sonar running constantly was slowly depleting her freshly charged batteries. While she still has plenty of reserves, she never knows when she's going to need them. The circle of light's still quite a bit off from the strength of daylight on Earth, but considerably brighter than the faint UV-glow–for which she needs filters–in this frigid, shrill, helium-filled layer. Is it light from the next layer seeping through, or merely a mark for the South Pole gate?

The next uncertainty is the set-up of the next opening. If it's a shutter timed like the first one, then she might need to have to wait two hundred and thirty-three days. That seems next to impossible, in this environment. If it's an actual opening of the same size, she should be able to pass without incident, as she's lost some mass through the fired mini-torpedoes and the use of her ion thruster. However, if for some reason it's tighter—more restrictive—she might go down in spaghettified flames.

The gravitational signature of the whole alien object is immensely complex. Gravity waves superposed on gravity waves, gravity waves of all kinds interfering with each other, and more. On top of that these gravity waves are weak, so in order to measure them in all three dimensions a carefully aligned, laser-operated network the size of a solar system is necessary. A bit too large for her to take along, as it is.

So she can only do a few indirect measurements through a number of sacrificial probes. As they get ripped to their atomic components, they do confirm that the gravitational 'safe passage' in this opening is the same as in the very first one (within the measuring error). While the temptation is large, she doesn't want to fly through the circle of light. Safety first, as there is no immediate hurry.

One of the secrets humanity managed to get about the inside of the Enigmatic Object—at a price that Na-Yeli can barely imagine—was that the openings between the inside shells were not like the outside 'shutter'. While supposedly the same size—which Na-Yeli just confirmed—the inner gates are reported to be like a strange kind of permeable membrane, a Diaphragm Gate if you wish, that filters out everything except sentient biological matter and everything in contact with it. Dead matter, machines, or even machine intelligences would find those Diaphragm Gates as impenetrable as the barrier shells. Relatively simple biological life forms like plants, lichen, or fungus would also not get through. Sentient life forms, and most definitely self-conscious life forms—and everything in contact with it and not further than twenty centimeters away—would pass, taking into account the size of the gate.

Assuming these data were correct, humanity developed hybrid drones, in order to allow Na-Yeli to take a 'sneak peek' into the conditions of the next layer, and—if necessary—make preparations. The actual drones are uplifted Kitti's hog-nosed bats—the smallest bats known to humanity that barely survived the Anthropocene—fully integrated with the most advanced drone machinery. They can be cloned easily, making it possible for Na-Yeli to produce new ones if the original ones are damaged beyond repair, or lost.

In honor of their origin, Na-Yeli calls the hybrid, sentient drones 'Kittis'. Right now, she has ten of them. Because they can–hopefully–traverse the diaphragm gates before or after Na-Yeli, they don't count against her maximum mass limitation (only when she crosses the shutter, and when she has to do that the second time around it means she's on her way back home, and this has become a luxury problem). Assuming there is useable material in the other layers–she most certainly doesn't want to hunt or scavenge the life forms in this frigid helium layer–she doesn't need to cannibalize from her own.

Now is the time to find out: can her Kittis pass through and return? Can she pass through? Na-Yeli strongly believes these gates will be traversable, otherwise, there is no point to this whole object. Whatever its secrets, whatever its surprises or unique environments, they're all useless if they can't be reached. Deep inside, Na-Yeli thinks there is a method to this madness, and she's intent on unveiling it, no matter what it takes.

So she sends out a few Kittis to see if they can get through the, well, rabbit hole to the next layer. She programs them for a five-minute reconnoiter in the next layer. As fast as she can see, they pass through the membrane–which is opaque, yet somehow seems impossibly thin–without a problem.

Five minutes later, they return. They've measured an atmosphere about twice as thick as the helium frigidscape she's still hovering in with her vacuum balloon. No radioactivity, same fast-rotating electromagnetic field, slightly stronger gravitational pull–all things that are not unexpected.

Their camera recordings do indeed show a strange wonderland beyond the semi-permeable rabbit hole: multi-hued reflections from glassy structures that shine with an eerie grace. Those are some ten to twenty meters in the distance, so there should be sufficient space for flying. According to their measurements, the gravity is still small enough, and the atmosphere thick enough for her to hang-glide through.

It seems safe to enter. Question is, will that transparently thin, flimsy diaphragm let her through, as well? She's already calling it a semi-permeable membrane, or Diaphragm Gate. Only one way to find out.

She rides a long, upswing thermal and then positions herself stack above the middle of the circle of light, then gets into a fetal position as the form-fitting craft reverts to a sphere, then steers it straight down the middle, accelerated by the one-twentieth G pull of whatever mass there is stack in the Enigmatic Object's center. Approaching the passage, she notices that the Diaphragm Gate's semi-permeable membrane reflects her oncoming image, and does she see a slight ripple before contact ...

THE FRACTAL MAZE

*T*hrough the second rabbit hole, Na-Yeli thinks, her pressurized exoskin preventing her from feeling the atmospheric pressure increase, *five more to go if the shell structure is regular.* And regularity is what she gets in the next layer, regularity at almost every level. Repetitive, self-similar structures everywhere in full, multihued geometric glory. Yet their colors vary. Vermillion branches on mauve trees, yellow buttresses on purple castles, intricate ice flowers with blue petals, scarlet stamens, and viridescent stems, too much to take in at once.

In the realm of the fractal queen, she thinks, *so pretty after the dullness of the helium grayscape.*

Exquisite castles of crystals, enticing spirelets of stalagmites, and ethereal silhouettes of stalactites. Lightning flashing in an almost staccato rhythm. Icy structures, menacing like Mandelbrot nightmares.

Icy structures like snowflakes squared, fractal-like tendrils growing out from massive pillars, branching out all the way into atomic realms. Icy structures like transparent trees on acid with an inner light show.

Crystalline edifices of all shapes, kinds, and sizes. Stalactites growing up from the nano-scale to mountain-sized: microscopic needles, barely visible mounds, tall pillars, small hills up to huge mountains. Complemented by their mirror-image cousins: stalagmites growing down from an invisible ceiling, almost-but-not-quite fitting with their floor-bound kindred like the closing maws of a planet-sized crocodile.

Their growth guided by the whims of random chance, symmetry, and iteration. The crystalline complexities arise from both the bottom and the ceiling. Na-Yeli has no idea how the latter is possible, but the glassy, fractal structures drooping from above almost touch their crystal counterparts from below. Yet, spread very irregularly, there are the odd mergers—columns where stalactite and stalagmite unite—and maybe these are strong enough to hold up the immense ceiling, in this micro-gravity? But this throws up a chicken-and-egg problem; for the columns to form, there had to be a ceiling. So then what held up the ceiling in the first place?

The whole layer is like one huge cave, there is no big sky to fly through. And while the numbers of columns and other mergers between floor and ceiling are relatively rare, the stalactite heavens and stalagmite netherworlds often approach each other so close she can't fly through these narrow passageways. She has to carefully make her way in an unpredictable fractal maze. Thankfully, the atmosphere is thicker than in the helium dogfight layer–pressure about 60% Earth-normal–and the gravitational pull, while increased to 0.074 G, is still so gentle that gliding on thermals is quite easy. And flying–even if she takes the long way around–is multitudes faster than walking (which could also be quite treacherous).

In the meantime, her sensors and spectrometers dutifully analyze the atmosphere, finding it an almost fifty-fifty mix of ammonia and carbon dioxide. Temperature a chilly one-hundred-and-fifty degrees Kelvin. Anyway, there is light. *Without the constant lightning that also continuously recharges the near-ubiquitous instances of both phosphorescence and fluorescence*, she thinks, *it would become pitch-dark in here.*

The reflective signals from her radar and sonar have become extremely complex to the point of being indecipherable. Her lidar has gone haywire the moment she has jumped through the opening in the South Pole. Reflections of far-off structures are reinforced by similarities closer by, while reflections of nearby structures are diminished through absorption. It becomes well-nigh impossible to use them to determine if something is close or in the distance. So line-of-sight it is, a much lower load on her batteries.

But line-of-sight is unreliable, as well, as fractal structures look similar over a wide range of sizes, wreaking havoc with her sense of depth. So she flies slowly, not helped by the turbulence that seems to occur randomly and often brings her dangerously close to the fractal tendrils of all types of crystalline growths. The razor-sharp fractal tendrils, as confirmed by the maximum zoom of her combined camera equipment.

On the one hand, her exoskin's metamaterials are tough. On the other hand, she only has a limited amount of them. There, another turbulent bump, and her right wing inadvertently touches a crystalline fractal branch, causing a rip in its outer layer of metamaterials. They are self-repairing, but a small bit did get scraped off. She can't keep this up forever.

Then there's the lightning. There's a ton of electricity in this layer: static charges, direct and alternating currents, electromagnetic swirls and eddies, interference patterns with fractal signatures. Na-Yeli's betting that these also power the lavish light show. Sharp fluorescent oranges, reds, and yellows. Soft phosphorescent greens and blues. And bright white flashes reflected and refracted everywhere.

The static discharges flashing between the various crystalline structures aren't the worst, as they always try to find the path of least resistance. Na-Yeli is relatively safe if she stays in large gaps. Intuitively, it seems similar to the uncertainty principle; that is, the larger the gap, the smaller the chance of a lightning bolt. On the other hand, the lightning bolts that do cover large distances are the really powerful ones. In full Faraday cage mode, her craft can take a certain amount of lightning strikes. But she has a nick in her right wing already, so she wants to avoid the really big electrical discharges.

Unfortunately, they have huge siblings, the enormous lightning strikes from the hazy clouds that drift throughout this fractal maze. Followed by a slow thunder that seems to reverberate for long, long seconds.

After the chilly serenity in the previous layer–even if it was spiked by vehement dogfights–the light show in this veritable fractal labyrinth becomes overwhelming. At first, it was a nice change of scenery, but the constant attack on her visual senses has become wearying. She's reluctant to put up filters, as they might make her miss seeing some crystalline fractal tendril that, when she scrapes past it, might open another tear in her metamaterialistic armor. Some are large enough to spear her, outright. Some are large enough to land upon if their fractalized surface didn't look so bloody sharp.

She's been underway for over fourteen hours–including her passage through the treacherous, frigid neon layer–and hasn't had a chance to sleep. Fatigue is rearing its heavy-lidded head. But there's no way to fly on autopilot in this highly unpredictable terrain, and she hasn't seen a landing spot she trusts, just yet. Maybe it will come after the next turn, after the next crystalline structure, bombarding her with a myriad of colors. If she could just stay out of the way of all the lightning, large and small, flashing in all its stroboscopic irregularity, thank dog. A recurring pattern might have been hypnotizing.

Fatigue worsened by constantly battling the turbulence of the volatile atmosphere. It would be great as a joyride in an interstellar amusement park, but Na-Yeli has stopped seeing the fun in this. She's tired, bone-tired, dogfight-tired, and just wants to rest, but sees no opportunity for it. *If this is just the environment*, she thinks, *I shudder to think of what aliens it will host.*

Her attention wavers and there, another scratch after touching a crystalline, fractal tendril, sharp as a million mini-razors, again on her right wing. The pain peaks through her fatigue, but this is not the right way to stay awake.

The constant barrage of light, geometry, and rough atmosphere is also not enough to keep her awake. Deep exhaustion sets in, no matter how hard she fights it. She could use some exquisite drugs–or medicine, depending on your point of view–to stay awake, but is extremely reluctant to do so. Not because she's afraid of side effects and possible addiction, but because of the precedent. If she has to resort to extreme measures already, barely at the start of her long expedition, then what can help her if things get even harder, crazier, and more challenging than this?

She doesn't dare sleep, she doesn't dare to land, and a vacuum-balloon will be swept everywhere, inevitably experiencing a puncture. Something has to give. She's been falling in and out of short bursts of sleep in mid-flight. She must touch down, but nothing, really nothing looks safe. She falls asleep again ...

... to be woken by a crash landing. She's hit the ground, a ground like a bed of nails, where the nails of the nails have nails, all razor-sharp. Some of her exoskin has been punctured, but not as much as she feared. She shudders to think what an Earth-normal gravity would have done to her inadvertent touchdown. She's hanging over a thick, fractalized crystalline branch at a worrying angle. She hurts all over her body, but emergency meds are releasing painkillers. She should check the status of her systems, but she doesn't care. All she wants to do is sleep, and as the painkillers set in, that's exactly what she gets.

eep within the REM realms, memories and dreams mix until they become indistinguishable ...

... she's small again, and young. So young daddy's still alive. She's gone into the kitchen, where she's told not to go to when daddy is preparing dinner. But does she listen? Hell no, because that was who she was, Na-Yeli the toddler, the obnoxious infant who had to learn everything the hard way, while being curious about, well, everything, as well ...

... "Na-Yeli, don't touch the conductive stove." Her mother—who followed her in—stern but with loving undertones.

"It's very hot," her father says, matter-of-factly, "you'll burn your fingers."

Na-Yeli puts up her unbelieving face, steps forward, and–of course–touches the stove. Her father doesn't stop her but lifts her as the burning pain sets in, and immediately puts her hand under the tap's cold water.

Na-Yeli cries her heart out, but her father is relentless: "I told you so. Maybe you'll learn to listen the next time."

Mother is much more comforting, kissing her on the head, making shushing noises as she applies a soothing balm. "Relax, baby, shush, everything will be alright," she says, "this lotion will stop the pain, will make your fingers good again." To her husband: "Why didn't you stop her?"

"It's the only way she learns," her father says, "otherwise she might have done it while we were away."

... in the next scene, she's just climbed out of the playpen barrier of her bedroom, walking towards the stairs with her uncertain steps ... she slips and suddenly the whole world becomes topsy-turvy– the ceiling's become the floor, the walls are sideways and everything is turning. It hurts, but the overwhelming feeling is one of wonder, weirdness, and wild abandon ...

... eventually, she rolls onto the ground floor, no wounds nor bruises, only a little worse for wear ... alarmed by the noise, her father and mother rush out of the living room ... Mummy terrified and immediately picking her up ... Daddy dryly remarking: "there's our little astronaut," which angers Mummy no end ...

... a big jump forward where she's doing all-important chemistry exam ... she's sure she nailed all the questions except the last one, the most difficult one ... she wants to nail that one, as well, and not only to show she's the best ... but also to show her father that despite her rebellious attitude, her pubescent temper tantrums and utter failure at being the nicest girl in class, her education, her learning, and her results haven't suffered ...

... but the solution is evading her ... how is it possible that the electric conductivity of a HCl solution is so much higher than that of an equally strong NaCl solution ... after all, the charge of both H^+ and Na^+ is exactly the same ...

... then she remembers that night when she was in utter despair at the injustice of it all, her father knocked on her bedroom door ... took her in his arms and told her she's not a failure ... that being small could be to her advantage ... "Sometimes, you'll see, when the going gets tough, and when things become very crowded, the smallest ones can move the fastest ... "

... and she sees it: the H^+ ions jump from H_2O molecule to H_2O molecule in a cascading effect that easily outruns the Na^+ ions that have to go *around* all these H_2O molecules ...

... she's got it, this should give her the perfect ten ... I never truly understood you, daddy ... so often you were aloof, so often you were hard on me, yet sometimes you opened up ... why did you have to go before I could learn to know you? So unfair ...

... even as the dream arrives at the inevitable realization–she lost her father in her last year of secondary school–it ultimately remains a happy one ... because she was with daddy again, if only in her dreams ...

Her intense dreams end the way they always do, as–nine hours later according to her internal clock–she wakes up. The pain in her bones, muscles, and punctured skin is gone, to be replaced by a massive migraine. She knows but all too well what that means, hoping it wouldn't be necessary this soon.

In her experience, the longer LateralSys is in control, the more intense the migraine will be–for her, the poor, slow CEO–afterward. Hence, the hyper-creative personality from her right brain hemisphere must have been busy for quite a while.

Her pod–well, she, the shape-shifting metamaterials of her exoskin with the assorted batteries, sensors, and equipment are basically one –is still static, but somehow feels better anchored, not in the precipitous position right after the crash.

As is her wont, LateralSys left a note in her computer implant:

Dear CEO of this very slow company,

Those were some nasty cuts and bruises in the hyper-advanced metamaterials of our exoskin. Also a decidedly *interesting* environment (by way of the ancient Chinese curse). I do understand that even a slow-witted Miss Egotrip like you must rest once in a while, but the way you parked the vessel was far from elegant. So I must assume it was an accident.

The crystalline growths–fractal to the atomic level–are extraordinarily sharp, indeed. And hovering like a balloon in this turbulent, lightning-laden environment is not an option. So we must fight fire with fire.

For this, I have used our lasers to melt some of those crystalline materials over a few metamaterial bars that I repurposed as landing gear. The melted crystal has the same hardness as the fractal crystalline tendrils, so our craft can settle down without a problem (as you may have already noticed).

I see that we're lost. I can't find our position, coordinates, or even some estimate by dead reckoning anywhere. A flight path that gives the craziest virtual joyride a run for its e-money, an electromagnetic field signature in this layer that gives white noise a good name, and a crystalline, fractalized environment that would fill the gods of chaos, asymmetry, and random chance with pride.

In other words, a challenge.

And you know how I love those. Here are my recommendations: use a combination of the 'touch-the-wall' technique and the 'pledge' solution–combined with visual pattern recognition–for conquering this fractal maze.

Touch-the-wall; that is, choose a 'wall'–for whatever your value of 'wall' in this sparkling, crystalline mountain forest–and keep following it, wherever it goes. This normally gets you out of any maze (with one exception, see my second recommendation), albeit not in the fastest way possible. But I don't think we have much choice in the matter.

The 'pledge' solution with visual pattern recognition is needed when the 'touch-the-wall' solution can be thwarted by a stand-alone part of a maze that is not connected to the rest, for example, imagine walls in the shape of the capital letter 'G'. Touching the wall of such a structure will let you do the merry-go-round forever. This is where the 'pledge' solution comes in. This checks if you've come back to the same heading–thank dog, the gyroscope's still working fine–again, while checking if you haven't made the same crossing by marking these.

We don't have the luxury of being able to mark each crossroad (let alone if such markings would stay long in this crazy environment), so we need to rely on visual pattern recognition. So let the cameras make recordings of the 'walls' we're 'touching' as we traverse this maze, and alert us when certain sections do look the same.

This is where the laws of chaos, symmetry, and random chance work in our favor: the chances of any two sections of these fractal structures being exactly the same are infinitesimally small. Also good that we didn't skimp on computer power and memory.

Enjoy the rest of the ride,

–LateralSys;

PS: I've also been able to reclaim some of the atomic constituents needed for our metamaterials from both the crystals and the atmosphere. But there are still elements we need, so do keep an eye out for them–I already programmed the spectrometers for this–so we can replenish the metamaterials lost.

PS 2: Sorry to take over just before you woke up–otherwise you could have slept off the migraine–but our body was much too tired to do anything after you crashed.

Na-Yeli feels elated with overtones of shame. A little bit ashamed that her left brain didn't think of these things, but she realizes that this kind of 'out-of-the-box' thinking isn't part and parcel of that particular hemisphere's set-up. On the one hand, she wishes that the brilliance of her right brain would be available at all times, but knows this comes at a cost, as the intuitive, artistic part of her is easily distracted and can get totally lost in shiny details, never mind if these are central to the mission or not. Hence the slow CEO is normally in command, as it can focus like nobody else–except when in overwhelming danger or exhausted.

In any case, she swallows a finely balanced broth that she can still think of as food–eventually, it'll be recycled excrement with added vitamins, minerals, and proteins–and as the migraine slowly recedes, she prepares to tackle this fractal maze, well-rested and better prepared.

Na-Yeli represents the human race, yet doesn't feel quite worthy. The judges of the 'Champion of Humanity' competition weren't offended when she revealed her self-induced tri-schizoid condition. On the contrary, they were well aware that she had an altered state and even complimented her on the extremely efficient usage of her brainpower.

Doubt, however, is a healthy part of her dominant personality. Still, knowing that doesn't alleviate her feelings of inappropriateness. Her other two personalities–LateralSys the right brain creative genius and KillBitch the subconscious survival machine–have no such doubts over their abilities, they're confident they're the best. Even then, her lurking personalities like to refer to her as 'Miss Egotrip' (for other, perfectly good reasons, but still) or 'the slow CEO'.

It was through a nascent 'double-blind spot'
hypothesis that *In the Gap of the Gods*–the research
group of which Na-Yeli was a member–eventually
developed the self-triggered tri-schizoid condition.
The general idea being that human minds, even as
they increasingly discover more about the reality
they exist in, might still have certain blind spots of
knowledge.

Derived from old learning methods and
theories, one could visualize a matrix:

Matrix	You	The Other
You	known knowns	known unknowns
The Other	unknown knowns	unknown unknowns

As such, they consider four areas of
knowledge. First, you–your mind–knows
the knowledge it already has: known knowns.
Second, The Other–another mind, this might also
be an alien–knows areas of knowledge that you
don't know: these are your known unknowns, or
the blind spots–gaps–in your knowledge that The
Other is aware of. Third, you are aware of blind
spots–gaps–in The Other's knowledge that they are

not aware of: unknown knowns for The Other. Fourth and finally, there are 'blind spots' of knowledge that neither you nor The Other is aware of: unknown unknowns, or knowledge that neither of you has, or even suspect exists.

Originally, our minds and their tools—qualia, intentionality, agency, cognition—were limited by our senses and the environment in which they evolved. Then, after we developed the scientific method and all its tools, we began to see things beyond what our limited senses could perceive, and we recognized many gaps—blind spots—in our knowledge that we are still in the process of, if not filling them in, then at least demarcating their boundaries.

The 'double gap' hypothesis suspects that there are still areas of knowledge of which we have no inkling because we cannot know them by definition. Opponents call this the 'black magic' argument, or a surreptitious way to sneak religious and spiritual beliefs back into the scientific method. However, many 'double gap' supporters are working scientists, and they truly wonder if there are areas of knowledge, logic, or mathematics that our brains physically cannot understand, that are beyond our brain's capacity to understand. Avenues of experimentation are machine learning, artificial intelligence, and the ongoing exchanges with extra-terrestrial intelligences.

The latter got started when First Contact was made, yet all the aliens we have met so far have not truly pushed our knowledge in new 'blind spots'. Even the massive, slow, time-reversed gas cloud intelligences of the Horsehead Nebula; the plasma patterns in Procyon-A, 1-Centauri and Kappa Tucanea; and the Von Neumann machine intelligences from Gamma Capricorni that seemed inscrutable at First Contact are now slowly opening up to our–increased–understanding. Only the rare few Moiety Aliens, who seem to be a rare occurrence to the other aliens, as well–as far as humanity can find out–remain a mystery. Then again, they are a mystery to everyone in the known Milky Way. Some even wonder if they are the secret builders of the Enigmatic Object.

Na-Yeli's group had two different approaches: outside→in and inside→out. Outside→in proposed that we cannot–by definition–fill in our unknown unknowns, that is: we need help from a *truly* alien perspective to both attend us to our blindness of blind spots, and–if possible–show us and teach us the knowledge in that double-blind spot.

Inside→out proposed the paradoxical approach, saying that our minds and brains, even if they did develop in a certain environment, are flexible enough to rise above that environment. After all, the scientific method had already demonstrated that, and there are no proven arguments that prevent our minds and brains from developing new types of understanding. So even if our qualia, intentionality, agency, and cognition seem self-limiting, the mind can develop new qualia, new forms of intentionality, fresh types of agency, and subsequently novel kinds of cognition that can open up new doors of understanding.

Na-Yeli's forced, self-induced tri-schizoid condition stems from the inside→out group. KillBitch represents her subconscious: a part of her mind driven by survival that–in order to keep reflexes as fast as possible–never developed self-consciousness, as that would slow it down. By design it is *not* conscious, and has only rudimentary means of communication–another mode it refuses to use as it slows her down.

LateralSys represents the artistic, innovative part of her mind, which is situated in her right brain hemisphere. It is the seat of her wildest imagination, the part that loves to think outside the box, to which lateral approaches are second nature. As with KillBitch, this heightened ability comes with a price, as LateralSys is easily distracted by beautiful things. Like a magpie unable to resist anything that glitters, she can get utterly lost in a sea of elegant details, never minding if she's drowning or not.

The Slow CEO–or Miss Egotrip–represents the rational part of her mind, situated in her left hemisphere. The logical, analytical part of her with a helicopter view over her situation. The part that carefully tries to consider all alternatives before making a decision, hence the 'slow' of the slow CEO. The part that is in charge most of the time, as it is not wont to get lost in an avalanche of elegant tidbits or keep killing everything around her just to show she's the top dog. Hence the 'CEO' of the slow CEO.

As such the slow CEO–who Na-Yeli thinks of as herself–takes all responsibilities for her actions, taking the blame if these decisions were wrong, and wallowing in the glory if these decisions were right. The latter earned her left brain part its second nickname: Miss Egotrip.

As it is, Na-Yeli reckons that the disdain of her lurking personalities is a small price to pay for their expertise when they are truly needed. So the triumvirate, the tri-schizoid personality persists, with the most important mission in the history of mankind.

Na-Yeli traverses the fractal maze with newfound hope. She has a plan, she has mostly replenished her material stocks and recharged her batteries and–thank dog–has not been attacked by aliens. *Yet*, she adds silently. While this layer is smaller than the previous one, the trajectory she is forced to take is much longer. If no aggressive aliens will show up, she might even take a few breaks, now that she has appropriate landing gear. A small part of her hates to destroy even a minor part of all that crystalline, fractal-till-vanishing-point beauty, but it's overruled by her practical part, the part that wants to survive.

The same practical part that programmed the autopilot in her computer implant to fly using the touch-the-wall rule. The same practical part that set up pattern-recognition algorithm that warns her when she passes terrain that has already been filmed. Even at the high resolution, they're using–Na-Yeli, if anything, wants to be certain–it will take centuries before her DNA-structured quantum dot memory is full. And the same practical part of her that reconfigured her magnetic compass–worthless in this wild electromagnetic environment, anyway–into a locator of the highest static charges, the places where lightning is most likely to strike.

Now that her mind is free to observe, and to wander, Na-Yeli must guard herself against distractions. Her improvised lightning predictor steers her away from the biggest lightning strikes, and the Faraday cage of her exoskin can easily take the odd minor bolt of lightning. The place has an almost mesmerizing beauty, like a semi-opaque coral reef made of multi-colored glass, but without the fish. She almost regrets the lack of fauna—while wondering if these crystalline, fractal-to-the-point-of-no-return edifices could be considered flora—until she recalls her vehement dogfights. Still, there could be benign aliens, as well?

As if in answer, she sees a twinkling that seems active, moving as she steers around a large, tapered crystalline stalactite. A shimmering outline of a looking-glass cloud. The multitudes of colors in this glass prison are constantly changing as she moves through the maze—different angles of attack, different angles of reflection—and she's been treated to so many refraction rainbows and diffraction prisms that they almost begin to look stale. But this is different, there is motion behind these color changes, almost as if there is a scintillating hint of life behind the twinkling. Possibly driven by the fact that the overall luminosity is never constant, always in flux.

She is tempted to investigate, very tempted. Does she dare lose the touch-to-the-wall, possibly negating all the progress she's made? Or can she start anew, hoping this won't take her back to where she came from? Then again, her pattern-recognition algorithm should warn her of that. Decisions, decisions.

Then the decision is taken out of her hand, as the glittering cloud is heading towards her. She's almost blinded as a massive lightning bolt strikes it, no—strikes right through it—as the afterimage confirms. She doesn't want to land, preferring to see this phenomenon from a higher vantage point. On top of that, while airborne she can get away faster if some kind of danger threatens her. So she settles into a figure-of-eight holding pattern, easier said than done in both the narrow crystalline canyons and the tempestuous atmosphere. But the sight is worth it, more than worth it.

The glittering cloud is a giant flock of—she can't find a better word—butterflies. Their serrated wings are transparent and seem super thin. *They seem so brittle*, Na-Yeli thinks, *yet their wings will cut like a molecular knife, I bet*. Gossamer wings of glass so delicate they deserve their own nomenclature: glassamer? The Glassamer Butterflies, cutting an erratic flight path through the turbulent sky, seem to reflect the myriad colors of their environment in

67

their own, delicate way. Or so it seems to Na-Yeli, who can't quite take it all in.

Then, as they come closer, Na-Yeli can discern it. They're not reflecting their environment like a twisted mirror, but each of them is displaying its own, colorful, ever-flowing pattern. One a living Mandelbrot gallery, zooming into brightly hued fractal patterns with no end in sight. Another features cyclonic swirls, hypnotic as primary colors fade into each other. A third meshes seemingly incompatible shapes into an Escherian tapestry. One even flashes a straightforward checkers pattern, with flowing colors: black-and-white, blue-and-yellow, grey-and-pink, red-and-green. Ongoing, in random order, as far as Na-Yeli can determine.

The more she studies them, the more it's true: each Glassamer Butterfly has its own, unique pattern flow. Ever-branching leaves; entangled strings on acid like the curly hair of a dozen Medusa's blowing in the wind; exuberantly blossoming flowers, petals, stamen, stigma, style, sepals, and all; exploding supernovae launching a never-ending stream of ejecta in a multitude of colors; watery waves in ever-changing interference patterns; crystal mountains rising through subduction forces, then crumbling to dust, reforged and rising again. She's bedazzled, dazed, and confused.

Their unearthly beauty seems unreal. *Why are they here?* If beauty is an intrinsic quality of the true workings of nature, then the Glassamer Butterflies are one of its most magnificent manifestations. As they come closer, Na-Yeli changes her course to keep a certain distance. Not because she's afraid of them, but because she's afraid to hurt them. They seem so delicate, so brittle. *I don't want to be the glass hammer that destroys them*, she thinks, *the hypnotizing fragility of beauty*.

It's a miracle that they survive at all, in this wildly turbulent atmosphere. Glass birds or glass balloons would have been thrown against one of the phosphorescent stalagmites or one of the fluorescent stalactites in these tempestuous gales. Yet the Glassamer Butterflies proceed just fine in the lightning-laden madness. Their flight paths seem erratic, random, chaotic. For every movement forward they seem to make three sideways, two up and four down. Or suchlike.

And while they seem to come dangerously close to the protruding, hyper-fractalized branches of this crystalline forest, the intricate extensions of this fractal cage; they never collide with them. Quite probably, avoiding her will be trivial to them, yet Na-Yeli doesn't want to put that to the test. She keeps her distance, films the wonderful creatures at the highest resolution of her cameras, taking in their sense of wonder with long, thirsty observations. *LateralSys will love this*, she knows, but the slow CEO, ever so reluctantly, returns to the mission.

She hasn't strayed too far from the last touch-the-wall point and as her pattern-recognition software acknowledges that she's back there, she continues with her trek through the maze. As she moves onwards, not meeting any threats or distractions, her mind wanders. How can this place be? How does it work? How can these stalactites hang down from above? What keeps the ceiling from falling?

The ongoing data stream from her improvised static charge locator–her old magnetic compass– gives a partial answer to her last question. While there are huge local variances–that catalyze the lightning strikes–on average both the upper and the lower crystalline edifices have a net negative charge. *They repel each other*, Na-Yeli thinks, *but this opens up a whole different can of worms.* How can a large environment like this have a net negative charge? Either charge conservation is wrong, or there's something she isn't seeing.

And all these hyper-fractalized branches, repeating patterns up to the atomic level: how do they grow? There is no flow of nutrients through those branches, as Na-Yeli would have seen that, transparent as they are. Even if some god-like intelligence had put them right there as they are, then the constant winds would have eroded them, and the ongoing lightning strikes should have left burn marks everywhere. Yet she sees only burn marks from static discharges that were recent, so recent she saw them happening before her eyes. And no signs of windswept erosion at all.

So these razor-sharp branches, both in the undergrowth and the upper foliage, must be replenished. But how? The whole sense of this layer defies her. What is it, this whole layer full of crystalline castles and fractalized forests? A giant computer of light? A chance structure arisen from the availability of the right materials at the right time? Then what powers it? Right now, the fool in her is asking more questions than the wise woman in her can answer.

She keeps flying through the maze, through turbulence and lightning, sometimes looping in upon herself–as indicated by her pattern recognition software–and then choosing the next wall before continuing. The fractalized crystals are beautiful, but there can also be such a thing as beauty overload. At first, it overwhelms the senses, but after a while, a certain acclimation sets in as she adapts to her new environment. She's afraid she's reaching the next stage, a type of ennui, a kind of tedium one experiences after having too much of a good thing. The way that weeks upon weeks in a tropical paradise with perfect weather makes one long for rain, or even snow. The way that eating the perfect fish taco day after day after day makes one long for a salad, a cheese sandwich, or a bowl of rice (or anything but a fish taco).

Hopefully, it's just her tiredness speaking, as she'd hate to lose her sense of wonder. Undeniably, though, at the moment the crystalline landscape's losing its luster, and she's but all too happy that the software can check and compare the structures of the 'wall' she's following, as she's lost the ability the distinguish the one from the other. Which is just as well, as she'd also have missed the next anomaly.

Somehow, the Slow CEO must have surmised this, as she's also programmed the pattern-recognition software to raise an alarm if it observes something out of the ordinary. Probably because Na-Yeli can't see everything at once, and she's mostly scanning the environment while trusting the pattern-recognition software will cover the wall. It's just raised the alarm, as Na-Yeli sped past that particular section.

She turns around to inspect what the fuss is about. The software superposes a red arrow indicating the anomaly over her vision, and even then it takes a while before her brain discerns it. An alien. A large, insectoid alien caught within the crystalline growth like a fly in amber. Strangely, it's located in the middle and near the top of a stalagmite rising from the floor in the shape of a near-perfect spire. *Like an alien pharaoh*, she thinks, *buried in a cone rather than a pyramid*.

She checks her database, but the alien is not one of the known species. Studying the rest of the cone, she finds some black discolorations that are not part of the normal range of crystalline hues, which –when observed from the right angle– might also be interpreted as symbols. Symbols like she has never seen before. Pointillist pictograms from one angle, transcripts from a topological quantum computer from another, or a three-dimensional shadow of a higher dimensional Venn Diagram at its most oblique?

Time to get professional help, and Na-Yeli activates the communication AI and tells it to scan and analyze the alien symbols. "Do you recognize them?" She asks. "Or can you translate them?"

–*implementing full database check*– the communication AI signals –*this will take a few minutes*–

Na-Yeli waits, while managing to squeeze herself around the stalagmitic spire encapsulating the unknown alien–the walls are very close by–in order to get a full 360-degree recording of the alien and its symbols.

–*no match*– the communication AI signals –*nothing we know about, but, of course, the universe is a large place*–

"Then what would your best guess be?" Na-Yeli says, slightly disappointed.

–*what looks like intricate art to us*– the communication AI signals –*might be mere doodles or clichés uttered by bored minds*–

"So you're saying it might be the alien equivalent of 'Kilroy was here'?"

–*more likely the explorer's graffiti for territorial markings*– the communication AI signals –*in other words, ET excreted here*–

"Yuck," Na-Yeli says, only partly joking, "you take away all the fun and mystery."

–*benny hill's version of occam's razor*– the communication AI signals –*in case of inscrutable expressions, probably the most vulgar version is true*–

"Now you make me wonder what Kilroy was doing while marking his presence," Na-Yeli says, "I need brain bleach."

After making careful recordings of the alien in crystal, Na-Yeli carries onwards. It's been a long day–for your value of night and day inside this alien object–and while Na-Yeli hasn't got a clue whether she's made good progress through this mesmerizing maze or not, she has to rest. She looks around for a landing spot as her eyes spot something strange, something interesting. Most of the time it seems static when all of a sudden–blink– two symmetrical lids go open and shut.

She gets closer, circling above it, noticing a small updraft, fading slowly. It reminds her of the giant mollusks she saw when snorkeling at Ningaloo Reef. A green-dotted blue body with a big, purple clam whose serrated edge is a bright yellow. It blinks again, like the nictating lids of an evil eye. Then Na-Yeli is caught in a vehement, hot updraft that completely sets her off course.

What in dog's name was that? Now she's really interested. She circles a little bit further away, just out of the path of the sudden updraft, and waits for the next nictation. Now that she sees it coming–its timing seems quite regular, once every four minutes–she quickly dives into the edge of the updraft and takes a few quick samples.

Her spectrometer measures tiny motes of silicon, sodium, and calcium, often barely bigger than a few atoms, encapsulated by proto-crystalline chemistry molecules like carbonates, oxides, and nitrates. *The seeds of this slowly–fractal by fractal–*

growing crystalline realm, she realizes, *dispersed widely through this turbulent atmosphere*. The highly active atmosphere induces massive static charges in both the upper and lower crystalline edifices, leading to electric discharges–lightning bolts from minuscule to massive–that also assist in keeping the atmosphere active.

Nevertheless, these processes consume power, and where does that power come from? One possibility is that it's somehow extracted from the Enigmatic Object's quickly rotating electromagnetic field, but Na-Yeli doubts it. *Quartz and crystals work fine with direct current*, she thinks, *but not with alternating electromagnetic fields*. It must be something else.

Na-Yeli lands on a spot not too far from the blinking clam, choosing it as her resting spot. But before she goes to sleep, she sends out one of her miniature probes, happy to find another use for her Kittis. She feeds it with the, up till now, very regular nictating schedule and with the mission to go down into its innards as far as possible, and record everything.

She launches it and follows its flight path as it approaches the Nictating Mollusk, then hovers next to it awaiting the next nictation. The purple-and-yellow quartz blink happens bang on schedule and the Kitti jumps into its maws like a suicidal insect diving straight into a Venus fly-trap. As the lids close, Na-Yeli immediately loses contact with her probe. *Dogspeed*, she wishes and waits a few nictating cycles.

At the first blink, she catches a signal from her Kitti, the Doppler shift indicating it's in, deep. The next blink she receives a very faint signal, from about twice as deep. At the third blink, she's lost it. She's tired, she can't wait all the time, and the tiny machine is programmed to come back when it hits a dead end, or after four hours of flight–its battery is good for ten. Her curiosity nags her, but the need for sleep is stronger and she nods off, in eager anticipation of the next morning.

Eight hours later, she wakes up to find that her proud probe has returned. *Good job*, she sends, even if she's not sure if the tiny hybrid's sentient mind can appreciate it. As she swallows the broth, trying to hypnotize her digestive system into thinking it is breakfast, she goes through the Kitti's data.

It's gone down quite far, a little bit over three kilometers. Then it must have come very close to the second outermost barrier, she thinks. Indeed, as the camera view from the probe gets darker the further it goes down–only a faint, ultraviolet phosphorescence providing some line of sight. Then the walls of the tunnel begin to emit a faint glow. *Probably piezoluminescence,* Na-Yeli thinks, *as these crystals are under increasing pressure from the weight above.* The probe eventually arrives at a sputtering light show that Na-Yeli remembers but all too clearly.

Spaghettification of molecular matter causing– among other things–triboluminescence, she thinks, *so the bottom barrier of this layer is slowly eating up the lowest stratum of crystalline matter.* But what is keeping the whole thing up? Essentially only the piping hot gasses arising from the spaghettification. Piping hot gasses that wish to go up. Piping hot gasses that are searching for a way out, seeping and brawling in every nook and cranny, permeating every crack. Until, at last, they do find a way out.

Somehow, opportunistic life must have formed around these vents, in the process becoming symbiotic. By controlling the rate of venting, the Nictating Mollusks prevent the build-up to extreme events. Too much pressure build-up will lead to volcanic eruptions with subsequent huge damage and possible extinction events. Too little pressure build-up and the weight of the whole crystalline layer might speed up the spaghettification, leading to an explosive build-up of pressure and even more massive volcanic eruptions. Keep the pressure just right and the whole edifice floats above (and below) the forbidding barriers.

Somehow, the process also charges the crystalline megastructure. Maybe–through the spaghettification process–the barrier absorbs (or otherwise removes) protons or positive ions, as these are heavier than electrons. Until the negative charge of the crystalline megastructure is so high that spaghettified positive ions are attracted–and absorbed–in there rather than in the layer's barriers, maintaining a certain charge in the process.

The crystalline megastructure that absorbed the electrons, caused–on the one hand–an increased pressure build-up until an equilibrium was reached, and–on the other hand–the repulsive charge of the inner and outer crystalline layers (up and down from Na-Yeli's viewpoint), thereby keeping the outer from falling onto the inner.

So the Nictating Mollusks keep this place alive, Na-Yeli thinks, quite the feat of alternate evolution. Like everybody else in the Milky Way–and possibly beyond–she doesn't know how old the Enigmatic Object is. Very old, for certain. Probably old enough for evolutionary processes to take place and establish various equilibria. Maybe this is the equilibrium for this place, not the realm of the fractal queen, neither the hall of the crystalline king, but the dominion of the Nictating Mollusks.

It's a working hypothesis, Na-Yeli thinks, *it'll have to do*. She gets up as the shape-shifting landing gear reduces itself to two soles the size of her feet. *Well, I hope it's a stable equilibrium*, Na-Yeli thinks, *as I don't want to be around here when the glass volcanoes start erupting*. She bends through her knees, jumps up, and switches on her ion thruster's afterburner, pedal to the metal until she can catch the first updraft. Gets back to the wall she's been figuratively touching and is on her way.

Another day where she can't be sure if she's taking the scenic route, or the shortest possible way. She suspects the former and sees no way to change it. She doesn't encounter any Glassamer Butterflies, wondering if they're rare. She does notice, now that she knows what to look for, several Nictating Mollusks. The colors and patterns are different from the ones she's first seen—yellow-and-black tiger stripes with white-and-diamond lids; red-and-white dappled boletus caps with viridescent blue lids; pink, twenty-fingered hands with caramel castanets—but their function remains the same. She made sure of that by circling near the first few specimens she found, awaiting the blink. Invariable, within three to five minutes, it came.

Maybe the timing depends on the length of the tunnel beneath it? She wonders.

She also notes that she's counted fewer Nictating Mollusks on the upper crystalline forests than in the lower one. While probably not statistically significant, it does give some support for her theory that there's probably less spaghettification happening upwards. It almost starts to make sense.

Then again, if these layers grow, fed from the destruction from below and above–recycling by force–then why don't they grow to each other, merging? So far, they haven't and Na-Yeli is glad about that. Last thing she wants is to run into a blind wall.

Yet she doesn't encounter a Crystal Curtain, but rather something else. A huge, bulbous creature, like six caterpillars merged at the tails, or a six-armed starfish mimicking a half dozen caterpillars. She observes it from, what she hopes is, a safe height. It moves, but very, very slowly. In its direct wake, the intensely spiky undergrowth is gone. The surface there is almost flat, gleaming with a glittery sheen varying from polished quartz to shining glassware.

So something is eating the undergrowth and upper foliage, Na-Yeli thinks, *and is this the larval stage of the glassamer butterflies?* Part of her wants to land next to it, and check how it can digest the razor-sharp crystalline branches. Is it melting them with its breath? Is it dissolving them with its stomach acid? The more practical, safety-first part of her decides to leave that an open question. It's probably not that important in the grand scheme of things. She carries on, making a mental note to check for these Starpillars before she touches down for rest. Most probably, her exoskin's metamaterials can withstand whatever these überlarvae throw at it, but she doesn't want to find out.

On her third day–by human reckoning–in the fractal maze, Na-Yeli spots two more Starpillars, one flock of Glassamer Butterflies– which she, with pain in her heart, only observes quickly–and a plethora of Nictating Mollusks. Nothing else she would recognize as fauna, flora, or otherwise living. Her flight path odometer tells her she's flown more than thirteen hundred kilometers. The shortest way from pole to pole in this level would be approximately one hundred kilometers, so either she's chasing her own tail, or the maze changes as she traverses it. It does change, as she carefully observed, but not quite fast enough for that. As despair threatens to raise its ugly head, she sees something in the distance, down below.

A spot of relative darkness in the always flickering, multi-hued light. A shallow cone of twilight, its base at the bottom of a deep valley, lit up by the circular ring of the Diaphragm Gate. It makes sense, as she had the feeling that the gravitational tug was slowly increasing, meaning she had to be going 'down'; that is, in the direction of the Core.

Coming closer, she sees that it's indeed similar to the Diaphragm Gate she went through in the previous layer. She's tempted to dive right in—oh well, after a heads-up from her Kittis, of course—but it's the end of her third day in layer two, and in here she can rest in safety. She calls it a night and decides to prepare for passage in the morning. As she waits for sleep, she can't help but feel that something has been observing her, all the time she was in the fractal maze. Of course, there's the almost palpable sensation of utter alienness throughout the Enigmatic Object, but she begins to suspect there are subtle levels of strangeness throughout. *Like wheels within wheels in a spiral array*, she thinks, *possibly weird within weird in an inscrutable arrangement*, as sleep overcomes her.

A SEA OF HYPERWAVES

s Na-Yeli prepares to dive through the next rabbit hole, she wonders why the atmospheres of the separate layers don't mix through these openings. *A kind of semi-permeable membrane?* she thinks, *a kind of intelligent filter that lets life-sized objects through but not gasses?* In that case, fauna from each layer would be let through, and then, most probably, meet their untimely end. *Possibly evolutionary pressure has made the openings off-limit for native fauna,* she thinks.

As it is, prudence demands that she sends five probes through first, to examine what is in the third layer. What was the saying? *Only fools rush in,* she thinks, *where angels fear to tread.* Does that make her an angel? She suspects both KillBitch and LateralSys have a different interpretation. She programs five of her Kittis to do a quick in-and-out; that is, go through the transition, fly a full circle to survey the area, come back, and report. *So I can go in somewhat prepared*, Na-Yeli hopes.

They pass through the Diaphragm Gate and immediately Na-Yeli loses all contact with them. She waits a bit—she programmed them to come back after five minutes no matter what—but only one comes back, and already after two minutes. No other, not after ten minutes, not after fifteen minutes. Eerie.

The one that came back encountered a thick atmosphere and gale-force winds. The latter probably swept the other probes away. *Ye dogs*, she thinks, *I'm about to dive straight into a storm*. Now she curses herself, as she's slowly losing the courage to dive in. *So much for caution*, she thinks, steels herself, and bites the bullet. *I can't stay in the fractal maze forever*.

She lets herself be carried higher by an updraft, then heads down, speeding up as fast as she can. *If these winds in there are really so strong*, she realizes, *then they might slam me against the barrier if I don't pass through fast enough*. Speed is of the essence. She rushes to the opening as straight down as she can possibly get, mentally crossing her fingers, thinking *Oh my dog, oh my farting dog*.

She pierces through the Diaphragm Gate, straight as an arrow, eyes open, hoping she won't crash into something. She's hit by a very painful shock, like a massive body slap starting at her head and moving down over her body to her feet, at exactly the same speed with which she's diving through. *The pressure increase,* she thinks, too late, *I should've doubled my internal pressure to match.* The moment she's through, though, she's swept into the madly rotating wall of the craziest vortex she's ever seen. Hurricane-force winds push her into a path that's spiraling outwards. She doesn't want to go there, and she needs all her hard-won flying skills to push herself inwards. Struggling with all her might, she manages to break through the eyewall into a relative pocket of tranquility.

The eye of the passage and the eye of the hurricane didn't align, she thinks over her intense pain, *that's for sure.*

In the meantime, her instruments and sensors aren't sitting idle. 95% N_2, 2% CO_2, and 2% O_2, supersaturated with 1% H_2O vapor, her spectrometer reports, with traces of NO, NO_2, H_2O_2, H_2S, O_3, and Na^+, Ca^{2+}, Cl^-, SO_3^{2-}, SO_4^{2-}, H^+ and O^{2-} ions. Pressure: 205,000 N/m^2, or about twice Earth-normal. *That's the body slap I got when entering,* she realizes, as the pain slowly recedes, *twice earth, but with much less Oxygen,* she thinks, *too bad, as I would have loved to get some fresh air into my recycling unit.* If she filters carefully, she can still do that, though.

On top of that, she needs to prepare better next time, as she could have increased her internal pressure before going through the gate. Then again, after overthinking it, she might have lost the courage to dive through. And she only wants to invoke KillBitch—or LateralSys, for that matter—when absolutely necessary, because using them comes with a price. After a KillBitch episode, she's utterlyy exhausted, and she greatly prefers to enter a new layer well-rested, *if* she can help it.

There is light in this layer, visible light with a subtle red tint. Na-Yeli's search program hunts through the encyclopedia in her triple-redundant quantum computer via her implant and finds a match. A gas-phase reaction of chemiluminescence: $NO + O_3 \rightarrow NO_2 + O_3$. This delivers a visible broadband from red to infrared light. *Not as crazy as the non-stop light show in the fractal maze*, Na-Yeli thinks, *nor as dark as in the helium layer*. Good.

Right in the center of the vortex—the proverbial eye of the storm—she's orienting herself. A massive circular wall of clouds rotating around her like crazy. Everything seems to be circling the same vortex. *Well, at least that explains where my poor Kittis went*, she thinks, *swept away like voices in a hurricane*.

Above, the outer barrier, where droplets of water are reduced to Hydrogen and Oxygen while burning right back into water again, visible as pale blue sparks against the dark heavens. Sometimes, as the vortex shifts through the unpredictable powers of physics and random chance, the circular light of the Diaphragm Gate appears into view.

Down, way down–about five kilometers, according to her instruments–a churning sea. Or at least it looks like one. Zooming in, it appears that the wild waters below also form a vortex, albeit of the maelstrom kind. *A large body of water, by the looks of it*, she thinks, *makes sense, as all this water vapor has to come from somewhere.*

Conceivably, she could turn her shape-shifting exoskin into a floatation device, some kind of boat, even. Looking at the roaring waves below, where the mighty whirlwind turns into a messy maelstrom, she thinks it's not a good idea. *Well, it's very windy at the pole*, she thinks, *maybe it clears up further south. Way down south*, she corrects, remembering the fast-moving clouds on the far horizon.

While performing a figure-of-eight holding pattern in the eye of the storm, Na-Yeli considers her options. She likes to study her environment and get an idea of what makes it tick–might always come in handy, might prevent nasty surprises–but she also has a mission. Roughly speaking, her mission is to find out what makes the whole

Enigmatic Object tick (and by extension, possibly what makes the whole Universe tick), and studying everything in the separate layers would be tantamount to getting lost in the details. While she did have plenty of time in the fractal maze, as she was forced to take the long way around, she might be able to take a shortcut here.

Why fight the storm, she figures, *if you can ride it?*

Option 2 is to get down to the water level, improvise a boat-like structure, and sail from the North to the South Pole–that is, if the sea (the huge amount of Na^+ and Cl^- ions in the air make it likely that the water is salt) does go on all the way to the South Pole–but the waves swept up by this storm will not make it a nice trip, to say the least.

Option 3 is to get down to the water level, and turn into a makeshift submarine–after all, if she can survive in a vacuum, so she can underwater–and travel below the waves to the other side of this layer. While she may have to get into the water at some point anyway, traveling underwater is much slower than flying through an atmosphere, especially an atmosphere so close to Earth-normal as this one.

So she prepares for option 1: ride the storm. It'll be a wild ride, for sure, but with some luck, it can cut her travel time quite short, at least in this layer. Back in the solar system, they've taken her through several category 5 hurricanes before sending her through the edge of Jupiter's Great Red Spot, with four-hundred-and-fifty kilometers per hour winds. She can take some punishment.

Her plan is straightforward. She'll speed up to the highest velocity she can get, then dive into the eyewall as lateral as possible–as they trained her on Earth and Jupiter. Then enter the vortex, then spiral away from the vortex until she comes out of the storm. Once out of the storm, she can head straight South, taking the shortest route to the South Pole. If no crazy local creatures attack her, she can then dive down in the water, turn her shape-shifting exoskin into a submarine, and head for the opening. Easy come, easy go. So things will get rough at first, but should eventually calm down.

She comes out of her holding pattern in an ever-widening spiral while accelerating. Then checks if there are no crazy things ahead, and makes contact with the eyewall. Initially, it's a blast, even as the shocks she gets from 'scooping' the storm's inner barrier are quite severe. Yet the most advanced shock-absorbing foam humanity can make is taking most of the true sting out of them. She rides the storm–*your speed is for nothing,* she sings inwardly, *and your energy for free*–her speed increasing to a few hundred clicks, tempestuous winds throwing her around, yet nothing she can't take. So far, so good.

But as she spirals ever more outward, the storm remains fierce. She approaches the 66th parallel–the Arctic Circle if you want–and the storm shows no sign of abating. If anything, it's increasing. So far and not so good.

She does a few quick calculations. Here in the third layer from the outside, the outer diameter is one-hundred-and-seven kilometers. Storm systems on Earth, let alone Jupiter or Neptune can be–and, like the Great Red Spot and Great Dark Spot often are–much bigger than that. *Oh shit*, she realizes, *the atmosphere of this whole layer is probably one huge storm.* So far and *oh my dog*.

She's doing well over five hundred kilometers per hour already. *If this goes on*, she fears, *the winds at the equatorial region will be insane.*

And it does go on. Spiraling outwards from the 66th parallel, the wind speeds only increase. Not only the wind above but also the waves below, she sees to her dismay. The highest wave ever recorded on Earth–a tsunami crashing into Lituya Bay in Alaska–was well over five hundred meters. *Surely, they can't get that high in here, right?* Na-Yeli tells herself, against her better judgment, *a smaller body of water, no time to build up sufficiently.*

Her eyes tell her differently. As the wind speed exceeds one thousand kilometers per hour, the waves keep getting higher, as well. The winds are now so strong that she cannot turn back. Even at maximum power, her ion thruster cannot overcome the immense gale forces. Like it or not, she's committed to, what seems, a one-way trip straight into hell. *What have I done*, she rues, *why didn't I take the serenity of the submarine trip?*

At the 44th parallel–about halfway between the Arctic Circle and the Tropic of Cancer–the winds she's riding make a class 5 hurricane seem like a tempest in a teapot. About twelve-hundred-and-fifty kilometers per hour, but not quite Mach One as the air pressure is twice Earth-normal. It's closer to the Tropic of Cancer that things become supersonic. *About Mach One for this environment,* she reads on her instruments, *winds exceeding the sonic barrier.* She's tossed around like crazy, but her shape-shifting exoskin has expanded while filling the space between her and her outer hull with the best shock-absorbing foam known to man. It's extremely rough, but so far she hasn't experienced any major damage. Mentally, though, she's never been so scared. *Oh my dog, the winds at the equator will be close to Mach One point Five*, she thinks, *the worst is yet to come.*

She doesn't know the half of it. If the super winds at the equator won't be her end, then there's something else rising to finish the job. It's impossible to miss, even for a Na-Yeli hanging on for dear life. The sea level was almost five kilometers under the upper barrier at the North Pole, as measured by her radar, sonar, and lidar. Obviously, in this wildly rotating madhouse—Na-Yeli is now completing a full turn in twelve minutes— there will be a considerable flattening at the poles, and a subsequent bulging at the equator. So let's say the distance between the average sea water level and the upper barrier at the equator is approximately three kilometers.

Then she looks at the height of the waves below her as she crosses the 23rd parallel or this place's churning Tropic of Cancer. She can't believe her eyes as her gaze turns south, towards the equator. *That's not possible*, she thinks, *they're reaching all the way to the ceiling*.

For a few moments, her mind switches from 'scared-to-death' mode into 'sense-of-wonder-squared' mode. *That's not possible*, she thinks again, yet is unable to discard the evidence before her eyes, *this is the most awesome thing ever*.

A perfectly symmetrical row of waves, sixteen of them, all curling in upon themselves like surf about to crash, circling the equator in thirty-six minutes.

With a circumference of almost three-hundred-and-thirty-six kilometers, that equates to about five-hundred-and-sixty kilometers per hour. All of them, without exception, seemingly scraping the ceiling, the upper barrier that is the roof of this layer. *It's scary, yet I don't know why*, she can't help but sing, *'scuse me while I touch the sky*. And in the red-tinted sky, the waves are indeed purple.

A teetering train of tsunamis on the brink is the best explanation the scientist in her can come up with, synchronized to perfection and self-reinforcing like a resonant vibration. An undulating sequence of soliton waves sweeping through the sea snake Ouroboros who's realized–too late–that it's been swallowing more than it can contain, and yet somehow doesn't know its current situation is impossible, like Wily E Coyote sprinting like crazy above an abyss in the precious seconds that it doesn't realize it should fall. Eventually, gravity brought the resourceful, yet unlucky coyote down. Why hasn't gravity, even at 0.125 G, brought these stupendous solitons down? Or did Na-Yeli just arrive at the moment of this crazy system's suspension of disbelief, before it all comes crashing down?

In practical terms, though, it means her untimely end, even if she survives the full strength of this mother of all hurricanes, this top dog of all typhoons. If the top of the waves does make contact with the ceiling, she'll be squashed like a bug, or, more correctly, pulverized like an ant under an elephant's foot. Even if there is a hand's width space between the waves and the roof, she'll be pushed against the upper barrier and spaghettified at five-hundred-and-sixty kilometers per hour. *Atomized by the finest cheese grater ever*, Na-Yeli's turning to black humor, *unfortunately, nobody from the Guinness Book of Space Records to witness this.*

This is an enemy even too big for KillBitch, while LateralSys is too busy appreciating the incredible beauty of this all. It's up to the slow CEO to find a way out of this, or come up with the best last words as she circles this layer at one-seventh of an RPM.

If she's lucky, very lucky, stupendously lucky, she might stay between two of the hyperwaves as she circles the equator. But she has almost no control over her position, nor her speed, and will most likely either be hit from behind or thrown into one head first.

Head first? a desperate scenario for survival unfolds before her mind's eye, *what about I go down as fast as I can get, and then use my ion thruster to push myself into the wave before me.* Once inside the wave, she must swim down, down, and down while maintaining the same rotational speed as the wave, until she is below the very bottom of the wave, into the deep blue sea itself.

There will be a massive undertow and dog knows what kinds of eddies and vortices, Na-Yeli thinks, *but let's face it, it can't be worse than this magnificent nightmare I'm in right now.*

To the very best of her abilities, she maneuvers down as she positions herself in between two hyperwaves, massive walls of water hurtling along at tremendous speeds. Initially, she wants to get in at the middle—she estimates that there's a twenty-one-kilometer gap between the hyperwave tops—when she finds that the super-hurricane winds already want to push her into the wave in front of her. *Of course*, she realizes, *the wind pushes the waves, but the waves will not go as fast as the wind*.

Meaning she would have been pushed into a hyperwave anyway. However, that would be near the top, as the fastest winds are near the top and the thermal updrafts naturally push her that way, as well. The top is the place she wants to avoid, so the best tactic is to enter just before an onrushing hyperwave, then fire her ion thruster's afterburner so that she goes down, as far as possible while the super-hurricane winds push her to the hyperwave in front.

Down as fast as she can before she gets too close to the utter madness of the equator, slowly getting closer to this aqueous uprising to end all uprisings. Down in a relative way, as she's already moving with a humongous speed. Maintaining an aerodynamic shape in the direction of the wind, so that it's pushing her as little as possible, trying to reduce the speed difference between her and the wall of water as much as she can, while going down. Luckily, the wind speeds decrease as she goes down, slowing her down to well below one thousand kilometers per hour.

She sees the wall of water coming closer and–at the last possible moment–reverses course and goes against the wind, with all her might. Her speed decreases to nine-hundred, eight hundred, almost seven hundred kilometers per hour as she hits the wave. She's managed to reduce the speed difference to under one-hundred-and-fifty kilometers per hour, yet the impact is still massive. But survivable.

Alive by dead reckoning, she thinks, *now swim with all I've got.* Again, everything is relative. If she doesn't swim down, but down and too much forward or afterward, she will swim herself out of the wave to an untimely end. While dead reckoning may have saved her, a wrong live estimation may kill her.

Down, I have to go down, she tells herself, *but not out,* as she desperately swims down in this surf of the titans, this soliton wave of the gods. She estimates that she has about two kilometers to go before she is out of the wave and into the deep blue sea. About a thirty-minute swim if she equals the world record for 800 meters freestyle, which she can top because she does have all the enhancements professional athletes are forbidden to use. Thirty minutes will be almost one full rotation at this parallel, pure madness.

But that's not all. If she can get down, she has to prepare for the immense pressures at the bottom of the sea–where the opening of the South Pole will be–as well. She mentally programs the shape-shifting metamaterials of her exoskin to form a one-seater arrangement with a hull of syntactic foam blend of tiny glass spheres and epoxy resin that stands up to the extreme pressure, floats, and allows her movement, because she has to swim. Swim for dear life.

She uses all she's got, pushes herself and all her enhancements into the red, and touches a cold, irresistibly strong undertow after thirty-one minutes. She doesn't have the power, nor the will to fight it, and lets herself be carried along, waiting for that fateful moment when she'll be thrown out of the water, into the mother of all storms. But it doesn't happen. She stays underwater, breathing a heavy sigh of relief.

Not that Na-Yeli has come at rest underwater. However, since there are no scrambled-to-the-point-of-white-noise electromagnetic fields in here—like in the fractal maze—her compass and dead positioning (another function of the dead reckoning software) equipment have a fairly good estimate of her position in this third layer. She's been dragged around quite a bit, albeit at a much lower speed than above. Her equipment kept track, and as she is now moving with, what she calls, the undertow, she can extrapolate a rough overview of the underwater flow patterns.

While the mega storm and the hyperwaves rotate clockwise—in the same direction as the Enigmatic Objects fast-rotating electromagnetic field—the undertow acts as under a series of cells. Just below the surface these cells—Na-Yeli wanted to name them 'supersonic cells', but the water movement speed is well below the sound barrier—follow the clockwise rotation, but at the break of each wave their flow goes to the bottom, then turns back to a counter-clockwise movement before going up again. Hence these cells all have clockwise flow, as well. Yet the undertow beneath the cells has a counter-clockwise rotation.

The undertow is about two kilometers deep, much too deep for any of the chemiluminescence at the surface to shine through. It's pitch dark. Fortunately, the crazy flows seem to disperse the closer she gets to the bottom, and by tacking a bit against the stream, she uses the force of the flow to get deeper. She's still north of the equator, making counter-clockwise loops that take about two hours to traverse a full circle.

Going deeper, the power of the stream gradually disperses, until–at about eight kilometers deep, three kilometers from the bottom–she can finally swim, so that she can go in a direction she wants to. The shortest way to the Diaphragm Gate at the South Pole–which, she has to assume, will be strong enough to prevent the sea from emptying itself into the next layer–is about thirty kilometers. At a brisk pace of one hundred meters per minute, that's still five hours away, supposing she can keep going that long, which she probably can't. Neither does she want to arrive there completely spent. There has to be a better way.

First, she extends her exoskin with two circular fins containing a grid of superconducting wires. The absorbed energy can be used for charging her batteries and–aha–propulsion. She considers producing a makeshift propeller, but the problems of making a shaft seal at this immense depth are well-nigh insurmountable. Instead, she chooses a more natural way of propulsion—the whale tail. Her legs aren't suitable for that, so her exoskin slowly, carefully—the pressure at this depth is immense—extends until it has a working mechanism, driven by a makeshift electromotor.

After some trials, luckily without fatal errors, she manages to get the whale tail going at a steady speed, propelling her with twice the speed she would normally swim. *About two-and-a-half hours to go*, she thinks, *if all goes well*.

As it is, Na-Yeli doesn't go as fast as she would like. At full speed, the makeshift whale-tail propulsion consumes more energy than her absorbing fins extract, and she doesn't want to arrive at the opening with almost depleted batteries. Enlarging her charging fins is also not an option, as they will then greatly increase her resistance, and cause the whale tail to use even more energy. After an hour of trial-and-error, the size of her charging fins and the motion of her whale tail have been optimized. The only way to arrive with fully charged batteries is simply to move a bit slower.

She doesn't mind, as it gives her time to recover after the utter madness—and unparalleled awesomeness–above the surface. She already prepares a plan for the reverse journey, if she comes back and if that immense equilibrium state still exists at that time. It's darker than outer space– no stars in this underwater environment–and much colder than at the surface. The latter doesn't bother her, as the insulating qualities of her exoskin are near perfect.

As her battery's energy levels increase, she considers setting up a big searchlight upfront but thinks better of it. Both her sonar and radar notice nothing for several hundred meters around, so she'd only be illuminating empty water, or worse, advertise her presence to potential predators. *Nah*, she thinks of the latter, *they'd all be blind, anyway.*

Nothing much happens for a few hours. While all seems quiet, Na-Yeli can't suppress the feeling that she's either being followed, or observed, or both. She's now within fifteen kilometers of the South Polar gate, according to her instruments' best estimate, and is trying to figure out possible problems with the transition. The pressure at the very bottom of this layered sea is about one-hundred-and-twenty bar. If the pressure at the other end is one bar, or lower, then several highly unpleasant–to say the least–phenomena might occur.

For one, her exoskin–now perfectly withstanding the immense pressure–will expand quite a bit. More than enough to make get her stuck within the one-meter opening (if it's the same size as the previous ones). Even worse, there might be shock waves erupting from the compressed part of her to the uncompressed part as she moves through the opening, squashing her feet while exploding her head. More than sixty times the reverse of what happened when she entered the two-bar atmosphere at the top.

She sees no easy solutions. She may have to set up an underwater enclosure around the opening–a fortified dome, a kind of underwater igloo–then lower the pressure in the dome, and then go through. But where does she get the materials for such dome, and then support it? The barrier will spaghettify its foundation! There are dissolved metals and minerals in this sea, but filtering them out will take ages.

So while she'd like to get to the South Pole's Diaphragm Gate via the most direct route, she needs to do some reconnoitering. *Typical*, she thinks, *I'm prepared to meet all kinds of aliens and all types of challenges, and then overcoming the pressure difference at the bottom of an inner ocean might be the most formidable obstacle yet.* But she's not about to give up, far from it. She's only in the third layer, dog knows how many more to go, let alone going back out. In the long view, she's barely started.

Therefore, she changes her route: instead of swimming for the South Pole in a straight line, now she follows–as far as the often hyper-fast undercurrents allow her–in a large spiral with a two-hundred-meter diameter, hoping to find something, anything that can be used as dome material.

About two hours later, she's rewarded for her new strategy, which includes moving away from the calmest parts of this turbulent ocean, as it's in the fast-moving undertow that she finds echoes of life. Very faint ones, at first, as her sonar–her radar's microwaves are too easily absorbed underwater, and her lidar has a limited reach for the same reason–only barely detected them.

Yet Na-Yeli is willing to follow even the vaguest of hints and hits jackpot as she moves towards the indistinct sonar reflections. It's far from easy, as the life forms she eventually discovers move against the fierce undercurrent, and it takes quite some power and effort to get close to them. But it's definitely worth it.

Screw-Worms, is the first thing that comes to Na-Yeli's mind, *a school of vermian species spiraling against the stream.* The subsea life forms have a long, tubular body like worms, yet a thin membrane–let's call it a strange kind of fin–runs around the tubular body in the shape of a screw. A dark screw brightened by yellow stripes and spots. And even then, she's only able to distinguish this screw-shaped fin after she replays the footage of them caught in a long lidar burst in slow motion.

She finds them utterly fascinating, and studies them for a while, noticing they change the pitch of their screwfins by stretching their tubular bodies in order to maintain a more or less constant rotation speed as the flow of the undercurrent varies. *Like old-fashioned wind turbines,* she realizes, *they maintain their RPM at different wind/water speeds.* Probably because whatever they do, works most efficiently in that particular RPM range.

However, she can't study them forever, and has no choice but take the next step: catch one and dissect it. While the Slow CEO is not exactly squeamish, she still has the kind of conscience that tries to minimize the loss of life. Unfortunately for that single Screw-Worm, bigger things are at stake.

The dissection shows even more interesting things. For one, the Screw-Worms perform chemosynthesis, for example, $12 H_2S + 6 CO_2 \rightarrow C_6H_{12}O_6 + 6H_2O + 12S$. The carbohydrates they produce are partly broken down and reused for growing their tubular bodies, while the Sulfur–in combination with Calcium Carbonate–is used for expanding the screw fin, providing the yellow stripes and spots. Through some freak of random chance or evolution, their preferred RPM not only produces the lowest sound footprint but acts as a sonar absorbent, as well. Which makes her wonder: stealth from what?

The fast rotation of the Screw-Worms—they do spin incredibly fast—also generates heat which powers the chemosynthesis. *These creatures are the algae of the deep seas*, she realizes, *so I can't be the only one after them, right?*

Their nervous system is rudimentary at best, so the single Screw-Worm she dissected probably hasn't suffered pain. Which is all for the best, as she needs to catch quite a few more. For starters, she produces a strong and versatile net, then catches the school she's been studying. She calculates the mass of Screw-Worms she caught and the amount she needs for a pressure dome. Not quite enough, so she continues in her search for more catch.

In the midst—well. more like a quarter—of her trawling expedition, Na-Yeli encounters a distant echo from her sonar. It's both quite clear yet quite far away, so no sonar stealth capabilities should be involved. Since developing stealth capabilities is a survival trait, here in this deep black sea, she's suspicious. Is it a trap? Yet, her innate curiosity compels her to check it out, if very carefully.

She heads towards the echo's location, and the sonar footprint becomes ever clearer and larger as she approaches it. It's relatively big and also relatively unmoving; that is, it's in that rare place where all the ocean currents–and some of these can be quite turbulent and ferocious, Na-Yeli knows from experience–cancel out, a kind of unique calmness not unlike the legendary Sargasso Sea of yore. And also like the actual legend of that place (whose veracity has never been confirmed), it seems to have become a 'Graveyard of Ships'. In this case a necropolis of space pods.

Remnants of previous expeditions that failed, Na-Yeli thinks, *interesting, but that's not what I'm here for*. On top of that, she's certainly not the type to dance on her competitors' graves. *However*, she realizes, *plenty of useful materials*. More than sufficient for the pressure dome she has in mind.

Yet she doesn't go to the Hyperwave Sea's Graveyard of Spaceships directly, but approaches it in a circumspect manner, taking a few long circles around it in an effort to detect any predators or– who knows–those who lay in wait for her to take the bait. Recognizing ambushes was an important part of her training. However, after the most careful checks she can come up with in this Stygian Sea, she finds nothing. So, with all systems ready to make a run for it if things go astray, she moves towards the galactic debris site.

Then, as the sonar reflections become so sharp that she begins to discern separate vessels, but these are rather nondescript, probably because most of her predecessors also used shape-shifting metamaterials, making it impossible to predict which final form they would eventually end up with. Then she sees why nobody would like to go there: two sonar shadows that clearly resemble Crabs, creatures infamous across the Galaxy. On cue, her Geiger counter begins to click, while they're still quite a bit away from them.

Bang-Bang Crabs are–supposedly–the survivors of a nuclear catastrophe (as it seems extremely unlikely that an alien species would settle there voluntarily). Symbionts–or parasites, depending on your point of view–that have integrated with nuclear-powered Von Neumann machines. Through an act of galactic pity, the Bang-Bang Crabs have been accepted in the Galactic Union of Species, which is why they've wound up here.

The planet Niflheim that orbits the sun Ragnarök is a total nuclear wasteland. The origin of the nuclear catastrophe is lost in the mists of time, only the result is visible: a planet whose crust and atmosphere are so saturated with nuclear radiation that it's deadly for almost every known alien species, with precious few exceptions. Strangely, though, not all activity had died, as the planet was crawling with a plague of replicating robots—crab-like Von Neumann machines—that, being nuclear-powered, constantly plow the planet's crust for fissile materials. In the process they release even more Uranium, Plutonium, and their ilk, worsening the already intense radiation. A nuclear greenhouse effect, if you will.

Then, somehow, the crab-like Von Neumann machines got infected with the sturdy remnants of the Niflheim's biological life—possibly mutated cockroaches, hyper-evolved scorpions, or others, it's anybody's guess—and the Bang-Bang Crabs were born.

The Bang-Bang Crabs stopped digging up nuclear materials willy-nilly, only doing so when their own was running out, and as a consequence, the planet's radiation reached a stable equilibrium. They also halted the replication process gone wild, and the Bang-Bang Crab population slowly reduced, as the symbionts either did not believe in or simply did not want to reproduce through replication.

They did so—inadvertently or not—by increasing their size until each Bang-Bang Crab had amassed a cache of nuclear fuel that was barely below critical mass (they probably found out the hard way, as a short, yet intense spike in the planet's radiation record showed). It was so successful that the population kept reducing, getting close to extinction level until the symbionts finally applied–or re-introduced–sexual procreation.

Normally, if two Bang-Bang Crabs came too close, the result would be mutual destruction as their combined nuclear caches exceeded critical mass, resulting in a nuclear explosion and its accompanying mushroom cloud. So they always kept their distance. However, as the nuclear cache of a Bang-Bang Crab ran through its half-life, its available energy decreased. Then, at the end of its useful life, a depleted Bang-Bang Crab would search out a congener in the same condition and they would mate. That is, the symbionts would clone themselves like crazy and the replication process would be allowed to restart for the shortest of times as the two nuclear caches were merged. Somehow, the combined nuclear caches were still above the critical mass, and the mating Bang-Bang Crabs would go out, indeed, with a bang.

The same bang that distributed miniature Crabs with their cloned symbionts over a wide area. The lucky ones that were able to mine new nuclear resources in time were the offspring that survived and kept growing just short of reaching critical mass. There is no intelligent species in the known Universe that does *not* make jokes about the Bang-Bang Crabs' sexual procreation.

Reminiscing about it brings a smile to Na-Yeli's lips. However, it also means that, due to the nuclear radiation, she can't use all that otherwise easily available material for her pressure dome. In the same way that the Sargassum seaweed–while simultaneously being the breeding place for European and American eels–supposedly smothered the old sea vessels of yore into the Sargasso Sea's Graveyard of Ships, the Bang-Bang Crabs' nuclear radiation smothered all space pods that wound up in the calm spot of this Stygian Sea.

No possibility to ransack this for elements, no use looking for survivors–the Bang-Bang Crabs radioactivity will have taken care of that–so Na-Yeli has no other choice than make a quick recording of this floating necropolis, and then continue with her fishing expedition.

Sometime later, she's slowly getting there. She's learned to discern the faint shadows of the Screw-Worms–there is one higher harmonic frequency that's still noticeable, if you know how to listen–and finds that going towards them, pushed by the stream they're spiraling against, is the most efficient way to catch them. Like algae and plankton, anybody or anything can just scoop them up, meaning they're flora that's still got a long evolutionary way to go before it can even think of becoming fauna. She's caught about half of her estimated quota when things go astray.

Seemingly out of nowhere, she's grabbed by powerful jaws and dragged down. The underwater predator has grabbed her in the middle, her head, shoulders, and legs are outside its grip. The infrared sensors in her exoskin of these parts notice the vague contours of a big, shark-like body with a long, thick, almost elephant-like trunk with a jaw that's caught her. The beast's eyes shine with an infrared glow, her sonar still sees nothing, only a short lidar burst outlining the true size of the predator.

Incredible, Na-Yeli thinks as she's stuck in the beast's maw, *an elephant shark with stealth capabilities.*

On second thought, it's a logical evolutionary advantage in these Stygian depths. Clamped by the Stealth Shark's powerful jaws, her arms are pinned to her sides. *What's it gonna do, chew me open and eat me?* she thinks, *good luck with that, my exoskin can take more than one thousand bars of pressure.* What she could have realized, though, is that this underwater predator would use a similar strategy like the bat-mats in the helium layer.

They go down. She–the prey–upfront. *Oh my dog*, she thinks, *it's gonna spaghettify me to death and then feast on my remains*. She's trying to think of a way, like an improvised hydraulic cylinder, to open up these powerful jaws. But before she can cobble something together she's slammed, quite unceremoniously, against the fearful barrier.

The metamaterials of her exoskin start to spaghettify. *Well, this gives a whole new meaning to the term bottom feeder*, she thinks desperately. It'll be moments, minutes at the most before her hull is breached and she dies from the extreme pressure. *Now only some spaghetti sauce and a feisty meal to seal the deal*, she thinks, dark comedy her last defense, before blacking out.

Yet Na-Yeli hasn't lost consciousness, as KillBitch has come to the fore. She needs to fight, but her arms are pinned down and her legs can't reach the Stealth Shark. Her most fearful weapon remains: her brain. Taking inspiration from the razor-sharp branches in the fractal maze, she quickly programs the tips of two of her mini-torpedoes to become pointed to the molecular–nay–atomic level. Quickly launches them, as her protective skin is spaghettifying away from her.

The mini-torpedoes make a sharp turn, then drill themselves deep into the body of the Stealth Shark, and explode. It does the job, the muscles of the mighty beast go slack, apart from its jaw that remains tight in a death grip, a final rictus.

Nevertheless, its tail stopped moving so now only its weight is pushing her against the barrier. KillBitch pushes against the barrier with her legs in such a manner that she and the whole shark still holding her topple over. As the shark's dead body hits bottom, she pushes again, liberating her body and the shark's trunk from the deadly barrier. The weight distribution works against her, though, and she comes down again.

KillBitch remains icy calm and keeps pushing off, trying to use different parts of her feet, in order to minimize the spaghettifying wear and tear. Keeps dancing this awkward death grip dance until she finally has the ion thruster in the right position. Then she fires it up: human exopod and Stealth Shark slowly rising from the fatal foundation. She keeps moving up until they're at a safe distance, buoyed up by a rising thermal. Then she leaves– KillBitch burns through energy reserves like nobody's business–and leaves it up to the slow CEO to get out of the dead beast's rictus.

Silently thanking the KillBitch part of her while simultaneously hoping that part will remain inactive for the rest of the trip, the slow CEO part of Na-Yeli improvises two cylinder-powered force multipliers while trying to ignore the pain, muscle cramps, and bruises that the fight for survival have left behind. Very slowly, at an infuriating pace, the mighty jaws with the triple rows of serrated, backward-pointing teeth open far enough for her to get out.

Out of the Stealth Shark's death grip, and out of immediate threats, Na-Yeli ponders how to proceed. For the dome she needs to fabricate, she can use the Stealth Shark's dead body as well. *If it contains sufficient amounts of carbon, I'm good*, she thinks, *as the metamaterials can work wonders with carbon*. A double graphene skin supported by the same syntactic foam blend of tiny glass spheres and epoxy resin that keeps the pressure out of her personal enclosure. On top of that, she needs to restock on matter for the metamaterials that were spaghettified during her struggle with the Stealth Shark.

Strip the shark of its useful material here, or at the opening? Neither is a good option, as she's likely to be an attractive target for other predators while floating quietly like a sitting duck. On top of that, discarding useless parts of the Stealth Shark's corpse—that will sink to the bottom—might attract scavengers that look for the signs of spaghettification. She prefers to be on the move.

So her best option is to remove the useful ingredients while she's moving–she's designing a number of intelligent strip-mining bots with highly miniaturized spectrometers that will move between her and the shark through a hollow tether–and then dump the useless part of the shark at a safe distance from the opening, to lure potential predators and scavengers away from the passage to the next layer.

I have to cross at least another twelve kilometers towing a dead Stealth Shark, Na-Yeli thinks, *and my sonar is useless against its kind.* So what does she have? Visible light might betray over a large distance–she can't assume these Stealth Sharks are blind–while giving her only limited sight. Then she remembers the Stealth Shark's eyes. They had an infrared glow. Anything that lives down here has to burn–or generate, like the Screw-Worms–energy, giving off a faint infrared glow. On top of that, the low wavelength of the infrared radiation doesn't disperse as much as visible light, so an infrared sensor would have a longer range.

Thus, Na-Yeli lowers the frequency–and energy expenditure–of her radar and sonar, and reconfigures her light sensors to be maximally sensitive in the infrared range. It gives her an immediate hit. *There, an infrared flicker, with a faint sonar beat,* Na-Yeli notices, *far enough to be unthreatening, and close enough to be able to follow me.*

She hasn't recovered enough to be going into another fight if she can avoid it. So Na-Yeli heads into a direction that's slightly away from where the Diaphragm Gate is—never smart to show your destination to your potential enemies—and, as her strip-mining bots begin their job, monitors the following alien closely.

It's barely visible, Na-Yeli thinks, *if it stayed a bit farther away, I wouldn't have noticed it. Does it* want *to be seen?* As she takes the semi-touristic route to the South Pole, the barely discernible alien presence follows her, always keeping the exact same distance. This slow-moving stalemate continues for a while as Na-Yeli, yet recovering, still feels weak. Then her infrared sensors notice a second presence approaching. Its infrared contours are but all too familiar to Na-Yeli. A second Stealth Shark.

Ain't it grand, she thinks, *I'm towing a dead Stealth Shark, am about to be attacked by a live one, with a third alien standing by for spectator sports.*

Then, to her utter surprise, the alien following her positions itself between her and the onrushing Stealth Shark. Its infrared signature becomes better defined, eight balloon-like lobes tied together through invisible tethers. *A Moiety Alien?* Na-Yeli's astonishment peaks through her fear, *They're even here?*

The Stealth Shark doesn't seem surprised, nor impressed. It simply attacks the Moiety Alien, its powerful jaws gobble up the forward four balloon-like lobes, then bite with all their might. This doesn't seem to faze the Moiety Alien, though–nobody's been able to detect any emotion in them, anyway, over many millennia–whose caught lobes, also called orbitals–don't break, show no cracks, and don't even change color as they stay pitch black.

Without further ado, its four free lobes shrink into nothingness while its four captured ones double in size. In the deadly silent waters, Na-Yeli hears a sickening crack. Then all eight orbitals return to their original size and the Moiety Alien moves out of the Stealth Shark's jaws, whose opening remains unnaturally wide.

With its jaw broken or dislocated, the second Stealth Shark decides to cut its losses and goes away. As its infrared signature fades into the cold underwater distance, Na-Yeli, still with the dead Stealth Shark in tow, faces the Moiety Alien with a mixture of relief and bafflement.

Thanks, she thinks, not knowing how to communicate with the alien, and *Why? They've never interfered with anything, ever.*

The first recorded observation of a Moiety Alien was well over twenty-five thousand years ago, in what humans call the Orion Nebula, by the Avuncular Hive Minds. Their appearance baffled everybody, except physicists studying electron clouds.

They always consist of eight parts: strange globules or lobes that look like falling water droplets. But instead of falling, these eight droplets have their tapered ends pointed to a single center. The tapered ends becoming so thin that for all intents and purposes, they are invisible at the very nucleus of the eight-orbital entity. Yet these invisible strings–even the highest resolution optical equipment couldn't discern them–keep the eight droplets–that looked like the orbitals of a carbon atom, multiplied by two–together, always.

What keeps these eight moiety-orbitals together? An applied Uncertainty Principle? A combination of quantum entanglement and quantum tunneling? Heterotic strings? Nobody knew.

Normally, these eight orbitals are exactly the same size. Hence the moniker 'moiety'. However, they can change the size of four orbitals relative to the four others. Always in proportion, that is, if four orbitals were shrunk to near-invisibility, the other four would be exactly two times as big. Again theoretically, it might be possible to let seven orbitals shrink into almost-nothingness, and the eight one would be eight times as big. But such a thing was never observed, as the Moiety Aliens always kept a certain kind of symmetry going. It could be linear symmetry, point symmetry, or rotational symmetry, and it was always perfect.

As they appeared in more inhabited systems, the myths and folklores of some of these visited alien species told that finding the home of the Moiety Aliens would lead you to the origin of symmetry.

According to stories that were either so old as to be labeled myths or so new as to be labeled rumors, the Moiety Aliens could change the color of their orbitals. While Moiety Aliens of different colors–expanding well into the infrared and ultraviolet–had been sighted, nobody had ever seen a Moiety Alien change color. Even more unverified reports talked about patterns appearing on the orbitals of a Moiety Alien, but even if that were true, they never used that supposed ability to communicate.

They were both the ultimate neutrals and the ultimate ciphers. They just were. Where they originally came from was unknown. Every other alien species had a home system, even the Horsehead Nebula's enormous intelligent gas clouds that were moving in anti-time–who found the Moiety Aliens, like most aliens, too small to notice, and who said that the Enigmatic Object had always been there, in other words: it would still be there in the far future–together with the extremely short-lived singular nanoflies feeding on Hawking radiation.

Nobody had any clue as to how they crossed interstellar space, they just showed up. Apart from their colors, they were indistinguishable at the individual level. They didn't participate in wars, they didn't use or steal resources, they didn't occupy valuable estate.

Some aggressive or careless aliens had opened fire on some of them. The orbitals that the projectiles, missiles or lasers hit always shrunk down to the invisible level faster than the weapons could destroy, or even impact them. If the explosions were powerful enough to destroy the– quickly doubled–bigger orbitals, the whole Moiety Alien popped out of existence, and seemingly popped up somewhere else, as if quantum tunneling. Because all the Moiety Aliens look exactly the same, nobody could say for sure that either the Moiety Alien at the explosion was really destroyed–although nobody ever found remains–and one of its kin merely pretended that its sibling had magically jumped through space, or that they did initiate a massive quantum tunneling event.

They didn't communicate. They didn't seem to interact with other aliens in any measurable manner. They just were.

They showed up in several inhabited systems, stayed there for a while, then disappeared. Were they the perfect drones for some galactic god? The ultimate tease? The mindless manifestations of some unknown principle?

Nobody knew. They just were. And then they were gone.

Na-Yeli is at a loss. She can't communicate with the Moiety Alien, who had just prevented a Stealth Shark from attacking her. After the incident, the Moiety Alien went back to her previous following position, just far enough behind her that Na-Yeli can vaguely distinguish it on her infrared sensors. *One thing at a time*, she thinks, *first I'll finish strip-mining the dead body. After that, we'll just see.*

In the next two hours, no other predators attack her. Her bots have transported all useful materials from the dead Stealth Shark to her—Na-Yeli's exoskin is now heavily bloated—and Na-Yeli drops the remainder some six kilometers away from the Diaphragm Gate at the South Pole, hoping that the inevitable spaghettification lures predators and scavengers alike away from where she—and assumedly the Moiety Alien—will be.

In the meantime, the slow CEO has figured out a strategy. *It's why I'm the CEO*, Na-Yeli thinks, *I might be slow, according to KillBitch, I might be egotistical according to LateralSys, but I have the overview, I plan ahead.* Now that she's survived two attacks—albeit one with help—Na-Yeli is happy that the Stealth Sharks are big. The first one—in combination with the Screw-Worms she already caught—has delivered her enough material to set up a makeshift pressure dome with the same structure and elements her own exoskin is using now. A syntactic foam blend of tiny glass spheres and epoxy resin sandwiched between two thin layers of carbon nano-weaves. A little bot factory, carefully bubbled out of her enclosing exoskin, is already preparing the separate segments, a bit like the ice blocks from an igloo. Once she has all the parts, together with a high-pressure pump with a series of non-return valves in its pressure line that leads outside the pressure dome, then she will finally head for the opening and try to build it up there as fast as she can, hoping to be finished and gone before attracting any undue attention. If she comes back, she'll probably have to build a reverse pressure dome at the other side, but she'll cross that bridge when–*if*–she gets to it. She's also figured out a way to, very temporarily, support her pressure dome.

Her horrific death struggle with the Stealth Shark also gave her some priceless data. As she was pushed against the deadly barrier, her instruments measured the rate of spaghettification (scientific research doesn't stop for urbane matters like life or death). So she's calculated that a concentric row of six thin yet immensely strong walls of carbon nanotubes could just do the job. Strong enough to withstand the forces resulting from the huge pressure difference, high enough to be consumed by spaghettification in about an hour, as the high-pressure pump needs time to pump out the surplus pressure. Her calculations also estimate that the pressure leaking in through the five concentric chambers–a labyrinth seal, in principle–is considerably lower than the pump will push out, meaning the pressure will be maintained as long as the pump keeps running. *Slow CEO, pah*, Na-Yeli thinks, *high-tech CEO FTW*.

Then there's the Moiety Alien, constantly following her, letting her know it's there. Since it's alive, it can probably withstand a gradual change of pressure. Na-Yeli doesn't think it has just popped in here, exploding into existence like a Boltzmann Brain, nor that it quantum tunneled its way in. *If it can quantum tunnel in here*, she thinks, *why not quantum tunnel straight into the very core, and extract whatever price is, or is not, hiding in there?* She figures it made approximately the same journey as her, finding its way through the layers. Now it is here, and most probably knows the immense pressure it's experiencing. Can it survive an explosive decompression? Most likely not, otherwise it would have left this place already. Remembering how it cracked the other Stealth Shark's jaws, Na-Yeli wonders of the Moiety Alien simply couldn't shrink four of its orbitals to minimum size, put them to the other side of the opening, then grow them to maximum size and pull the other four orbitals through? Maybe it can only perform that trick if the pressure in all of its eight orbitals is equal, or if something else is stopping it.

So it's stuck, and it doesn't want to go back. She tries to imagine herself in its place. Would she go back? No, not until she's explored each and every option, until exhaustion. She finds herself sympathizing with the inscrutable alien. *Caught between the devil and the deep black sea,* Na-Yeli thinks, *indeed.* And it did protect her from the second Stealth Shark. Na-Yeli performs a quick check. Yes, we both fit in the dome. As the size of the Moiety Aliens is well know, she probably, subconsciously made amends for it as she designed the pressure dome. *Let's build the dome first,* she thinks, *and see how we go from there.*

She builds the pressure dome, piece by piece, feeling a bit like an Inuit lost in an underwater world. She keeps it afloat above the opening, planning to get inside it once it's finished. While she's busy, the Moiety Alien is circling the perimeter, as if scanning for incoming attacks. After a frantic fifteen minutes, the building blocks of her pressure dome are micro-welded together and outfitted with their sacrificial support rings, ready to be put down. If she's fast, Na-Yeli could probably get under the dome and lower it before the Moiety Alien could get it. *Perish the thought,* she thinks, *I won't be able to live with myself for the rest of the trip.* How does she make contact with it? Nobody's ever done that before. Well, Moiety Aliens also never interfered anywhere before, so it's not the first precedent to be broken today.

Her infrared sensors easily pick up where the Moiety Alien is, and she flashes a beam of visible light at it. The Moiety Alien stops circling, and four of its orbitals point her way. *How do I communicate this*, Na-Yeli thinks, and then it strikes her. She flashes its visible light laser at the alien again, and then flashes it at the center of the opening, straight under the floating pressure dome. Repeats the sequence, a second and a third time until the Moiety Alien approaches, slowly. Carefully, it flows towards Na-Yeli, then past her until it is under the dome. *Excellent*, Na-Yeli thinks and quickly swims to the top of the dome. Aiming carefully, she pushes it down as her whale tail makes a few fast, powerful strokes, and then joins the Moiety Alien under the dome before the narrowing gap is too small.

Together they wait until the floating pressure dome touches down on the barrier, triboluminescent flickers of spaghettification burning up the sacrificial support rings announcing the very moment. Na-Yeli starts the pump and watches the pressure. One-hundred-and-twenty bar, one-hundred-and-ten, one-hundred, ninety, eighty bar. Initially, the pressure goes down quickly. Eventually, progress slows as the pressure difference the pump has to overcome increases. Minutes creep by as the pressure drops, below thirty bar, below twenty bar, below ten bar as the structure begins to groan, but remains in one piece.

If I calculated this wrong, Na-Yeli thinks, *the incoming pressure wave will kill us before we can get through*. The tense wait continues as the pressure drops, ever so slowly, below three bar. The Moiety Alien makes a very small move towards the opening and back. Repeats the movement several times.

Go in already? Na-Yeli translates, then shakes her head. *No, not yet*. She moves a bit up, and then down. *Not yet*. But it is time to do something else. Like she did before entering the sea of hyperwaves, she launches five of Kittis through the opening, hoping she won't lose most of them this time.

They wait for five of the tensest minutes of her life for the probes to return, as the pressure slowly drops to one-point-five bar and the sacrificial support rings burn up, becoming shorter and shorter. *If they don't come back*, she thinks, *we'll just have to take our chances*. But after four minutes and forty seconds, one probe pops back in. Its results arrive at Na-Yeli's computer implant. 1.1 bar atmospheric pressure, 69% N_2, 30.5% O_2, and several traces of noble gasses. Then the rest return with similar readings. *Jackpot*, she thinks, *let's get out of here before the lot collapses*.

She moves to and from the opening twice, hoping the Moiety Alien understands. Then she dives through.

THE BERSERKER FOREST

Even as her probe has reported a pressure almost equal to that beneath her pressure dome, Na-Yeli inadvertently prepares for the worst. Apart from a little slap, like diving into water, nothing happens. She looks behind, still wondering what technology keeps that immense wall of water out, and sees the Moiety Alien appearing from the transitional portal. First four very small, barely visible orbitals, quickly expanding to almost double their normal size. Then the Moiety Alien pulls its remaining, highly miniaturized orbitals through the Diaphragm Gate, moves down a bit as its lobes reshift to their normal size. *Good*, she thinks.

Na-Yeli falls through a hyper-oxygenated sky and spreads her arms, willing the metamaterials of her exoskin to form wings. Wings are formed, but they are too small. She's used more materials for the pressure dome than she originally calculated, and now she doesn't have enough left to form wings large enough to provide the lift she needs. On top of that, building the pressure dome as quickly as possible has drained her batteries considerably, less than thirty percent left. She can use her ion thruster, but only very shortly as her life support systems need energy, too.

While her instruments confirm the composition of the atmosphere as reported by her probe, Na-Yeli's cameras notice that she's in a twilight area. Darkness on one side, light on the other side. There is enough light to show that her downward spiral is taking her to a reflective ground level. Ice? The air temperature, at 250 $^\circ$K, is also below freezing.

Her downward spiral is accelerating, she's going down faster and faster. She hopes that a precisely timed burst from her ion thruster–which doesn't quite have the power to lift her, even at a gravity that's a quarter Earth-normal–will be enough to soften her landing. *Worked so hard to get into this place*, she thinks, *only to break all my bones at landing.*

Then she feels something under her wings, for circular pressure points trying to push her up. She looks below her and sees the Moiety Alien, trying to break her fall. While it can't quite lift her, it does arrest the acceleration of her fall. She's still going down fast, but not fatally fast.

Just before she touches down, Na-Yeli lifts her nose up and greatly increases the angle of her wings. This classic landing maneuver greatly reduces her horizontal speed–at the cost of almost all her lift–as she angles her legs down and fires up her ion thruster, hoping she times the burst just right. Her feet touch ground as her forward speed drops to below fifty kilometers an hour, this should be survivable. The ground is ice and instead of coming to an abrupt halt, Na-Yeli and the Moiety Alien–who stayed with her to the very end–glide over the ice, eventually coming to a standstill on an icy plain.

She puts up two thumbs in the direction of the Moiety Alien, knowing full well it's probably meaningless to it. *If we're going to be friends, maybe even partners*, she thinks, *we must learn to communicate*. No matter how rudimentary. So by repeating certain gestures after certain events, she hopes to imbue that meaning. They have to start somewhere, and a kind of gesture-cum-movement language it'll be. Now to get on with her mission.

If the ice remains as smooth as this, Na-Yeli thinks, *I could skate my way out of this polar region*. That is if the whole layer isn't one big ice shelf. But she did catch a glimpse of vegetation when she was still all the way up, closer to the temperate region. On the other hand, if the North Pole is also an ice shelf, then she may have to physically cut through it to get to the transitional portal there. She bounces a quick radar reading straight to the upper barrier above. Thirteen point seven kilometers, her instruments tell her. If this layer, like the ones before it, is also thirteen point seventy-five kilometers thick, then she's fifty meters up. She doesn't look forward to digging through fifty meters of ice—assuming the North Pole ice shelf is similar— but it could have been worse. *The average depth at the sea of hyperwaves was ten kilometers*, she remembers, *imagine that as ice.*

Na-Yeli looks at the Moiety Alien, hovering a few meters away from her, wondering where they should go from here. She still can't read the alien as its orbitals fluctuate in size, albeit gently as they slowly change colors, as well. Where they are, almost at the exact South Pole, the ice is quite flat and undisturbed. It seems to remain so in the half that's lighted by the unknown light source, far away. The ice is almost pure water, with precious few solubles, and as Na-Yeli has replenished her water reserves already at the sea of hyperwaves, she'd rather move onwards to a place in this layer where there are other elements.

Before we go, though, Na-Yeli thinks, *establish a simple yes/no protocol first.* She flashes her light torch at the Moiety Alien, then flashes it in the direction of the dark hemisphere, then points it at her face, very visibly shakes her head, and then walks a few paces in the opposite direction. Repeats it a few times, hoping to establish that a horizontal shake means 'negative' or 'no'.

Then she points her light torch to the Moiety Alien, then to the light hemisphere, then to her head and visibly nods her head, and then walks a few paces towards the direction she's indicated. Again repeats it a few times, hoping to establish that a vertical shake means 'positive' or 'yes'.

Then she waits a few moments, hoping these attempts at communication sink in, then points her torch at the Moiety Alien, and then in the direction of the dark side of the South Pole, and waits. A second later it moves to the left and the right a few times. Then she points her torch to the Moiety Alien and then in the direction of the lighted side of the South Pole, and waits. A second later, the Moiety Alien moves up and down a few times and then moves straight toward the light. Hoping she's established the rudiments for mutual understanding, Na-Yeli follows.

Their initial trip through the polar region is uneventful. For the first few kilometers, Na-Yeli has changed the metamaterials of her soles into skates and she's able to move at a brisk pace. The Moiety Alien seems to have no problem keeping up. *It probably could just fly to the North Pole and leave me behind*, she thinks, *the fact that it doesn't has got to mean something. Something profound.* Then the ice becomes rougher and covered with snow. So now Na-Yeli has turned her skates into skis, and the two of them keep going, albeit considerably slower.

The position of the far-off light source has also changed. *Whatever it is, it seems to be positioned right above the equator, and it's moving,* Na-Yeli thinks as her computer implant estimates how fast, *it makes a complete rotation in 24 hours and six minutes.* That's so anthropocentric, it gives Na-Yeli the chills. Then her analytical part makes a quick calculation based on the timing of the 'shutter', and indeed twenty-four hours and six minutes match 2^{165} Planck Times. Call it a cosmic coincidence.

In any case, it's impractical to keep following the light—the shortest way between two poles remains a straight line—so they keep going North. *This might imply a sleep cycle, if there's life in this layer,* Na-Yeli, at some point, has to sleep herself, *I might as well synchronize to it.* It also makes her wonder if the Moiety Alien sleeps, or otherwise rests.

As they approach the Antarctic Circle, the ice and snow are slowly making room for something that eerily resembles tundra. In the far-off sunset, Na-Yeli spots what looks like a small glacier. The terrain is not flat, there are hills and valleys. Even some undergrowth that might be the local equivalent of tundra vegetation, although it's mostly red. On the one hand, she needs to resupply her depleted elements. Since they're making such good progress, though, Na-Yeli doesn't want to stop to take a sample. *If that's flora*, she wonders, *will there be fauna?*

In the distance, there's something that stands out, in a literal manner. Gleaming white spikes from a common center. A local kind of spike bush, it seems, until Na-Yeli notices that it's moving. *An albino hedgehog*, Na-Yeli thinks, *how cute*. The animal turns its front towards Na-Yeli and the Moiety Alien as if it's just noticed them. She hears a sharp bark, almost like a battle cry, and sees the white hedgehog sprinting towards them.

The constant white glare of the icy landscape has distorted Na-Yeli's sense of distance. The albino hedgehog is quite a bit farther away than she thought, at first. Unfortunately, this also means it's much bigger than she estimated. As the pig-sized hedgehog sprints towards them like crazy, it takes one final jump and curls into a ball. The white spines–that are indeed quite sharp–bounce slightly on the frozen underground and then all Na-Yeli can see is a big, globular wall of white spikes rolling towards her at full speed. She's too astonished to step aside and is run over.

The spikes, while very sharp, aren't quite hard enough to pierce Na-Yeli's exoskin. She's pushed over backward and the morning-star-hedgehog rolls over her, not imparting any undue damage. Na-Yeli gets up, suffering nothing more but a few contusions and a bruised ego. The menacing hedgehog, after it comes to a standstill, seems disappointed that none of its spikes have caught something, and turns around for another attack. Before it can start to sprint, though, four of the Moiety Aliens orbitals have appeared under its soft belly while the other four, much larger orbitals are just outside the range of its spikes. It can stretch its invisible tethers quite a bit, Na-Yeli notices. Then the four small orbitals under the hedgehog increase to their maximum size, toppling the hedgehog over before it can start to run.

It rolls back on its feet, utters a loud bark of dismay, and prepares to attack Na-Yeli again. Once more, the Moiety Alien topples it. The scene is repeated, in slightly different variations, a few times until the hedgehog gives up and moves away. *Very kind*, Na-Yeli thinks, *and very smart*. The situation is resolved while nobody got hurt. Well, she is, but only a little bit and she deserved it.

Nevertheless, Na-Yeli's still baffled by how big it is. If that's a consequence of the hyper-oxygenated atmosphere, not unlike the Earth's during the

Mesozoic, then what other megafauna is waiting for them, especially in the tropical zone? Dinosaurs? Tyrannosaur Rex? Even worse? She's low on metals, hence also low on mini-torpedoes, mini-rockets, and the like.

But then she sees a rock, a round rock, albeit a rather fluffy one. For a moment, Na-Yeli's at a loss. What's special about a rock? Then it strikes her. They haven't seen a single rock in this weirdly anthropocentric layer, so far. Soil, yes. But not rocks, let alone mountains, as this layer–and the other six, for that matter–are simply too small for massive geological processes like subduction and rock formation. If it's not a rock, then what is it?

As Na-Yeli's curiosity is constantly piqued, she can't stop and investigate every little thing. The mission, she's gotta keep her eyes on the mission. *But even without a mission, whole Universities full of scientists across the fields could spend lifetimes studying all the weirdness in these layers,* Na-Yeli thinks, *alas, that's for the deluge after me.* They wish to travel onwards, ignoring the strange rock, but the strange rock won't ignore them. It sprouts eight feet, not unlike those of a huge spider, pushes its body off the ground, and goes after them.

What's it with this predilection for rolling, here, Na-Yeli wonders, *too lazy to invent the wheel?* She's too tired to run away–she needs to replenish the materials for her vitamins, proteins, and minerals the first opportunity she gets—and just lets this oversize spider do its worst, trusting her hardened outer skin. The rock spider tries to bite her with two fangs, but these slide off Na-Yeli's exoskin. It tries again, a few times, all unsuccessful, then takes its leave, making a few disgusted sounds.

Na-Yeli is too exhausted, and as something eerily similar to night sets in, she digs herself in, just below the permafrost. The near-perfect insulation of her exoskin should make her invisible to heat-seeking predators, but she programs five Kittis to hover around, checking for danger, for two hours each, the next one releasing the previous one. That should give her ten hours of shut-eye. She has no idea if the Moiety Alien needs sleep or its equivalent of a restoration-annex-memory sorting period. Yet it needs to get used to hers. It would be rather disappointing if it left while she slept, but there's only one way to be sure.

She's too deadbeat to care much. She's dug herself a nice bed and falls asleep in seconds.

She's at a gig with José, her first true love. The band, half human, half machine, blends brutal noise with stupendously tight, arithmetically complex rhythms and soaring soundscapes ranging from the impossibly divine to indistinguishable from white noise. If not for her, José probably would have left ... it's always her music, her movies, her restaurants that they visit ... his patience with her verges on the compulsive ... while there are short moments of undiluted love between the nights of wild lust and the days of silent misunderstanding, they're not enough ... this affair is not healthy, from neither side ... then why is she so bloody lovelorn after she makes the inevitable break ...

... but down, deep down, she's not ready, emotionally, for a long-term relationship ... after all these years, she's still not recovered from the unexpected death from her father in that faraway country ... night after night, she dreams that she can stop him from going on that particular business trip ... but she looks for him, in every corner of their house, in his office, at his friends, his favorite pub ... only to find that he'd just left, less than a minute ago ... she runs, runs, runs as fast as she can ... yet she never catches him, again and again ... the only man ... she'll never truly know ...

When she wakes up, bathing in sweat, she still feels slightly better as her nanomachines have scrounged some minerals and other volatiles from the environment, and the Moiety Alien is still there, waiting for her. They travel onwards, to the temperate zone and the tropics. A straight line from pole to pole is about ninety-eight kilometers, so she could get to the other side in two days walking if nothing untoward happens. She hasn't replenished enough for her metamaterials to develop a sufficient wingspan for flying-cum-hang-gliding. Walking is restful and gives her a completely different perspective.

Reminiscing about her new environment, Na-Yeli has a few sobering thoughts. She gathers that if the animals in the polar zone are already much bigger than their Earth equivalents, then the animals in the temperate zone—and especially the tropics—might be even bigger.

These massive animals, this megafauna is just too big to fight, Na-Yeli realizes, *we have to avoid a confrontation*. She programs the metamaterials to alter the appearance of her exoskin depending on its surroundings—which it can monitor through the myriad of mini-cameras that Na-Yeli carries. Like a cuttlefish in a coral reef, or more appropriately like a chameleon in a tropical forest, Na-Yeli blends with her environment, tries to become one with it.

While adjusting her camouflage, she shines her torch at the Moiety Alien and nods fervently. It can change the color of its orbitals but always keeps one orbital in one color. She doesn't know if it can change color on small sections of its orbitals. Yet she needs to find out.

The Moiety Alien moves up and down quickly in response, then comes to rest as its orbitals begin flickering, changing colors so fast its eight orbitals become one big blur. Then the blurring stops and they display quickly changing random patterns of black and white spots, like a cathode-ray tube of pre-interstellar travel times tuned to no channel at all. The blacks and whites become colors, the random changes become more orderly, and eventually, a camouflage pattern mimicking Na-Yeli's appears on the Moiety Alien's orbitals. *Very good*, Na-Yeli nods fervently, holding two thumbs up, *excellent*.

Blending with their environment as much as possible, Na-Yeli and the Moiety Alien travel onwards, straight north. Past the permafrost into the temperate region that starts quite barren and mostly mossy. Then the first signs of shrubs and trees–gargantuan ones, of course–and flocks of big birds crossing the sky. A large herd of grazers–a woolly crossover between horses and goats–feed on the tall grasses of the open meadows. They either don't notice Na-Yeli and the Moiety Alien or simply ignore them. No sign of predators, which is probably for the best.

Na-Yeli is strangely attracted to this layer. It's very Earth-like, yet when she looks close the differences become apparent and create a compelling cognitive dissonance—the moment she thinks she recognizes something, it's something else indeed. She'd love to study this strange version of home much longer, and in much more depth, but duty beckons. Oh well, maybe on the way back ...

The subtropical zone resembles a savannah with huge thorn bushes and impossibly tall trees near well-attended watering holes. The animals they see are similarly oversized—ultra-giraffes with impossibly long necks, a cross between a triceratops and a hippo with very thick legs she dubs Stomposaur, inflated elephants she mentally calls Zeppelinfants and four-meter long reptiles, not unlike Komodo dragons, whose huge farts are combustible, she amusedly calls Reverse Dragons.

But the megafauna is not that easily fooled. Except for sight, there's also sound—they are listening for them, and Na-Yeli does make a sound as she moves—and there's no smell—they're sniffing the air. While Na-Yeli's exoskin can isolate her from any environment, so she does not leave a smell, the megafauna then tries to listen for something that does move, but does not leave a smell (they've probably been there before, with other aliens).

As such, Na-Yeli—and supposedly the Moiety Alien, even if it floats silently through the air—need to be extra careful. It slows down their progress considerably, yet Na-Yeli suspects her footage will be worth its proverbial weight in gold, in these times meaning worth its terabytes in longevity elixir. Progressing slowly, carefully, they try to avoid the megafauna, which is easier said than done, as they move surprisingly silently. Their large feet in combination with the low gravity most certainly a factor in this.

They're getting ever deeper in the subtropics, where savannah and dense rainforests are interspersed. Clouds do form and rain does fall in this weird ecosystem, and not unlike Earth, some places are wetter than others. Na-Yeli and the Moiety Alien cross the edge of a rainforest that's still wet from the latest rain, evidenced by the gathered raindrops on huge, green leaves, as the occasional drip, drip of rainwater still falling from the trees, and the moist smell of fresh precipitation permeates it all.

Even if these dense rainforests are harder to cross, Na-Yeli sometimes wants to get off the savannah where—despite their camouflage—she still feels exposed. On the other hand, it's also easier for them to run into a local animal, but Na-Yeli rationalizes it by the assumption that it's mostly prey that'll be camouflaged like them, not predators. And she likes the change of scenery.

Initially, nothing strange seems to happen in this stretch of rainforest. Still, she has this uncanny feeling of a presence, of something that's there that she is not seeing. Or better, that she's overlooking, something that's so normal she ignores it, something that's hiding in plain sight. It's irritating, like an itch you can't scratch, but Na-Yeli just ignores it, as there are bigger dangers lurking.

Then the Moiety Alien starts to hum. That is, Na-Yeli hears a humming sound and scans every inch of the rainforest within sight, looking for, but not quite finding it. Frustrated, she wants to shrug it off and casts a questioning look to the Moiety Alien. Only then does she see that her alien friend is vibrating quickly, all eight orbitals of it and that this vibration is the source of the hum she's hearing.

Not much is known about Moiety Aliens, and nowhere in her database is a record of them vibrating and producing a buzzing sound. She tries to draw its attention, using several gestures that worked fine before, but it does not react. In the meantime it keeps vibrating, not quite enough to make Na-Yeli worry about its health—not more than she already is, anyway–but enough to render its camouflage useless.

She gestures to her friend to stop the shaking, but–if anything–its trembling increases as its humming rises in tone. *Even more noise and less camouflage*, Na-Yeli thinks, *as if it wants to be found*. Or–the more devious part of her offers–as if whatever phenomenon that's causing this, wants us to be found by the megafauna.

She tries everything to get through to her alien friend, even touching it–which she never even considered before–but all to no avail. The Moiety Alien's shaking increases further, and its humming becomes both louder and more shrill. If this goes on, even a snoring Stomposaur will hear it a mile away.

She's really worried now, not only about the Moiety Alien's condition but also afraid that some of the megafauna will burst upon the scene soon. Can she somehow tow her friend away? She starts preparing a makeshift rope and looks for the nearest exit as she suddenly sees it. There's too much white in this rainforest, she thinks, what gives?

Where she previously ignored the occurrence of mycelium filaments at the bottom of the odd leaf, she now sees it sprouting everywhere: between branches, covering trunks, stretching over bushes.

Neither did the odd mushroom or toadstool worry her much. But now there are toadstools, boletuses, and mushrooms, of all shapes and kinds, everywhere: puffballs and chanterelles popping up through the undergrowth–how did Na-Yeli get here without squashing any?–turkey tails on trunks, artist's fungus covering thick boughs, too many to mention.

What's this mycelium infestation, this mushroom invasion, Na-Yeli thinks, *El Fungi?* Somehow the Moiety Alien is under its spell, while she remains unaffected. These are not fungi occupying their ecological niche, but a veritable fungal take-over. Na-Yeli hasn't seen this many mushrooms since the single time she tried psilocybin tea. Countless white spores saturate the air as the myriad of mycelium filaments seems to envelop them like a cocoon. In the meantime, the Moiety Alien's vibrating like mad, producing a high-pitched whirr that would drown out your average helicopter.

This is getting out of hand, she has to do something, anything. How to fight this madness? The Moiety Alien isn't paying any attention to her frantic signaling. How to get it out of its fugue? Pull it away? Or … fight fire with fire?

She gets her most powerful floodlight and flashes it at maximum intensity at her alien friend. Again. And again. Is she imagining it, or is the pitch of its whirring lowering? She programs the floodlight to flash in stroboscopic pattern, first with well-established hypnotic patterns, then with their antitheses. It works, as the Moiety Alien's vibrations visibly lessen and its frantic noise dies down to a low hum. To finish off this madness, she slaps one of the Moiety Alien's orbitals, never thinking she would ever have to do that. To her utter relief, it returns to normal.

Then, all of a sudden, the overabundance of spores, mycelia, molds, and yeast-like infestations and all kinds of toadstools, mushrooms, and other fungi disappear. Also, as if by a miracle, no megafauna has noticed their weird—and often loud—behavior. Their camouflage is working again, and the amount of fungi in the environment seems normal.

Somehow, it reminds Na-Yeli of unconfirmed rumors of a solar system whose two habitable planets were dominated by an intelligent, planet-spanning network of fungi, which would annihilate anything resembling a mammal, irrespective if these mammals evolved there naturally or landed there in their space ships. Even in the space age, rumors, myths, and legends remain.

Then the Moiety Alien moves to and from her, its movement signals suggesting that *it* is worried about *her*. In her relief, Na-Yeli shakes it off as a side effect of its fugue. 'No problem,' she tries to gesture, pointing at herself, 'I'm OK'–two thumbs up–'but are you?'–pointing at the Moiety Alien, then wiggling her hands. It doesn't seem to remember its strange episode, at all.

But no time to reminisce about that, as they were just making such good headway. And they should now be paying attention to their surroundings, not to themselves. Na-Yeli shrugs– something the Moiety Alien has already picked up– and gestures that they should move on.

A s they're crossing a wide swath of grassland, the grass waist high, just not high enough to hide behind if she ducks. On the other hand, while she has to trust her camouflage, she can also see any megafauna from far away. Or, in this case, hear over a large distance. The silence is broken by two loud battle cries: one like the hiss of a thousand cobras, the other like the roar of a pride of lions. Looking in the direction of the noise, Na-Yeli sees two giants challenging each other.

The wise thing to do is to avoid this confrontation like the plague, make an evasive trek around it, and carry onwards. Na-Yeli knows she shouldn't do it, but her intense curiosity converts the immense battle cries into an irresistible siren song, and she does it anyway. She gestures to the Moiety Alien to follow her, and as they get closer, they witness a fight between an aggressive Stomposaur and a creature like a mix between a giant snake and a Tyrannosaur Rex.

The Snakosaur Rex walks on two legs that support a snake-like body, wide at the bottom while tapering to quite slim at the neck that, on the other hand, carries a disproportionally large head with huge jaws and large fangs. The thick tail providing a counterbalance for the surprisingly agile upper torso.

The Stomposaur–a bit like a cross between a triceratops and a hippo–has a large, rotund body carried by four fat, stubby legs. Yet it moves with unexpected speed, the chunky shanks almost becoming a blur. Its hippo-like maw carries a row of big, sharp teeth, while the triple horns on top of that maw glitter with an obsidian glare and are very finely pointed, indeed.

Na-Yeli missed exactly what caused the exchange of hostilities, but that they're angry at each other is but all too abundantly clear. They approach each other, the Snakosaur Rex letting out a hiss like superheated steam escaping from a melting boiler, and the Stomposaur roaring like the horns of a dozen cruise liners.

At first, they circle each other, letting out ever louder hisses and roars, and feinting attacks. Then the Stomposaur assaults, its triple horns leaving a row of bloody rashes on the Snakosaur Rex's left side. The huge reptile strikes back, its long and sinuous neck avoiding the massive mammal's gaping maw and sinking its fangs into its protruding belly.

Things escalate from there. The beasts are upon each other, striking, biting, and punching with blinding speed. Their fight becomes such a blur that the two brutes become all but indistinguishable, a battle cloud of epic proportions.

As it is, Na-Yeli can't help but wonder how fast these huge animals move. Yes, gravity is only one-quarter of Earth's. Yes, there is fifty percent more oxygen in the air than at home. Still, these immense monsters fight with such speed that Na-Yeli's quite happy to be out of harm's way.

As fast as it's begun, it's over. While the Snakosaur Rex is badly wounded, it still stands as it delivers its final bite in the Stomposaurs exposed neck. Quite probably, these fangs carry a poison as that bite didn't seem that deadly, yet the Stomposaur visibly starts to move much slower, losing its fighting ability.

Almost unnoticed by Na-Yeli–who was alerted by her outer motion sensors–quite a large amount of animals has congregated to, well, watch this fight. Even crazier, not all of these animals look like predators: there are several huge gorillas, some Zeppelinfants, a pair of Ultragiraffes–whose kindred were nibbling at the leaves of a huge tree the last time Na-Yeli saw them–and even a small herd of large grazers that look like a crossover between a llama and an antelope. The gathered predators–Stegosauruses and Reverse Dragons, apart from a few more Stomposaurs and Snakosaur Rex–do not seem interested in the very prey that's walking right between them. Curiouser and curiouser. Thank dog they show no interest in Na-Yeli or the Moiety Alien–either their camouflage works quite well, or they're simply ignored like the other prey–and they begin to get involved after the fight.

When the fight is finished, and the Stomposaur is beaten, the wounded giant is not eaten but towed along. And not just by the Snakosaur Rex, as it gets help from the other, gathered megafauna. They cooperate in a fashion that seems to say that they've done this before. Huge, gorilla-like bipeds enter the scene with what must be a huge net. Four Zeppelinfants wrap their long trucks around the wounded Stomposaur's legs and lift it. The Über-

Gorillas pull the net under the Stomposaur, whose expression seems to change from fear into a quiet kind of acceptance. The Stomposaur is put down on the net, and the Zeppelinfants, Über-Gorillas, Ultragiraffes, and other animals each grab hold—in their own way—of a part of the net, and together they tow the now deadly quiet Stomposaur along.

Na-Yeli and the Moiety Alien follow then as silently as possible, while Na-Yeli wonders what the Moiety Alien makes of this. She has no idea, herself, as her brain is trying to understand how this whole layer at large functions. She gets that the presence of a rotating mini-Sun generates a day-night cycle and that the mini-world somehow follows a near-similar evolutionary pathway to its own, twisted Mesozoic. But how does this mini-Sun work? It shouldn't be possible.

As Na-Yeli's mind tries to grapple with the world she's witnessing, she and the Moiety Alien are also—as quietly as they can—going after the strange parade of megafauna towing one of their mortally wounded along. The procession carries along, doggedly, working together to overcome obstacles, cross small rivers and make its way through the ever-denser vegetation. A collaboration in complete silence, hour after hour. Unwavering, unrelenting, and eerie.

As they follow the gathered megafauna, the savannah thickens into a tropical forest. The transition is sudden as if some freak event or some insane deity has decided that at this line savannah stops and mega-jungle begins. The whole layer must have an active climate complete with a water and carbon cycle. In the tropical region, the canopy of the thick, lush tropical forest is very high, and very thick, and almost everywhere of roughly equal height.

Except for a single spot stack on the equator where two towering branches from a single, forked tree stick out high above the canopy. It stands so tall it's visible from the edge of the tropics, some fifteen kilometers away. Na-Yeli can't escape the feeling that they're heading exactly towards that very point. She's having difficulties trying to take it all in–how does the ecology work? how can the megafauna cooperate like that? why would they?– and certainly won't get her answers today, as twilight calls.

The going gets much more difficult for the megafaunal parade in the thickening jungle, and inevitably evening sets in. At some point, as twilight fades into a starless darkness, the strange parade decides to set up camp by dumping the still barely alive Stomposaur in a small clearing, and then prepare for sleep in a circle around it. Na-Yeli and the Moiety Alien find a resting spot well out of sight, and Na-Yeli programs a sequence of Kittis to warn them when the parade continues.

To her delight, the soil is rich in nutrients, meaning her nanobots can replenish many missing minerals, metals, and volatiles overnight. Lost in thought, trying to make sense of this weird world, Na-Yeli eventually falls asleep. Not quite fitful as she's awoken several times by her Kittis and motion sensors, warning her for nocturnal animals passing close by. None of these are after her, or the Moiety Alien, fortunately, or simply do not notice them.

The next morning, the megafauna congregation has a sort of breakfast session. The herbivores forage for their preferred plants, while the carnivores hunt—some more successful than others—for small prey. Typically, the carcasses of the devoured prey are not discarded but thrown in the net with the poor Stomposaur, who's somehow still hanging on for dear life. Then the procession moves onwards.

The going gets pretty tough, but they're already quite close to their goal—the huge forked tree stack on the equator. *I knew it,* Na-Yeli thinks, *but, by dog, why?* They arrive just before noon.

The singular tree–the tallest one in the layer–
looks like a huge prong with two tips, its massively
thick stem rising until about two-thirds of its
height, which is about two-hundred-and-fifty
meters. Then it splits into two equal branches, like
a perfectly symmetrical fork. The massive tree has
only sparse foliage along its thick stem, and at the
bottom of its two forked branches. Halfway up the
fork ends, though, there is no foliage and the wood
has a black sheen as if it just came out of a forest
fire. Right next to that humongous tree, a
rectangular area has been cleared, the long axis of
the rectangle also stack on the equator, facing east.

Coming closer, Na-Yeli sees that two ropes are
tied to the fork ends. The ropes look thin in
comparison to the massive tree's two upper
branches, but in reality, they're thick, thicker than
mooring ropes of the mega cruise liners of yore.
The whole reminds her of something, but she can't
quite put her finger on it. *An oversized slingshot*, she
thinks, *Ah, that's it–a trebuchet.*

Close to the gigantic catapult tree, several dead
and severely wounded animals are laid together on
a huge leather pouch. The dying Stomposaur–
together with the bodies of that morning's prey–is
added to them. The two long, thick ropes are
connected to the sides of the pouch on one end,
and all the way up to the top of the two upper

branches on the other end. There's something in the air, a rising tension underscored by a low, sonorous, almost infrasonic wail.

The Ultragiraffes bend forward, their powerful jaws biting on the leathery strips connected to one of the many ropes that–looped under a curved, very thick branch that's anchored to the ground–all connect to the launching seat-cum-leather pouch of the enormous catapult. They bend through their knees, tensing the muscles in their four feet and mighty necks.

In perfect synchronicity, Zeppelinfants, Stomposaurs, Snakosaurs Rex, Über-Gorillas, Reverse Dragons, and other megafauna get a hold on the myriad of leather strips from the gargantuan sling, as well, and pull it back, exquisitely timed, as one.

Step by step the congregation of animals moves backward, gradually increasing the tension of the enormous sling. The moment the wounded animals in the huge leather pouch feel that they are lifted off the ground, they emit a wail that's as resounding as it is heartbreaking.

Yet the wail is not one with discord as the sounds synchronize and a song arises from those animals about to be launched. A dirge from the sacrificed, an elegy for the afterlife. Na-Yeli can't make out any words–if there are any–but the haunting melody brings tears to her eyes.

The premature requiem has a decided rhythm, a pulse perfectly in time with the steps of the congregation of megafauna who are tensioning the trebuchet. Yet it is not all doom and gloom, as overtones of acquiescence rise the fore with overtures of inception, almost as if the creatures of oblation believe in reincarnation.

In the meantime, the relentless tensioning of the trebuchet marches onwards, the two long ropes taut with a creaking assurance and the two forked branches bending over, backward to the ground.

The ritual started at noon, with the mini-Sun straight above the proceeding. As the mini-Sun is moving to the West, and the catapult horde moves to the East, there is no doubt as to where the gigantic trebuchet is aimed at. *They're going to shoot them into the mini-Sun*, Na-Yeli realizes, *any Aztec priest would be yellow with envy*.

Then the coordinated congregation reaches the end of the clearing, their muscles tense, rigid with vibration. The launching dirge reaches a climax and all the animals let go, as one, simultaneously.

The twang of the gigantic trebuchet is deafening, lashing through ear-drums and souls alike. The offering to be burnt is whiplashed into the sky on a trajectory of fate. Na-Yeli follows the animated load through her highest resolution outer cameras and sees that the orchestrated aim is true, as the heap of that animals–Na-Yeli certainly hopes the enormous whiplash has killed those still alive, as that would be preferable to being burnt up–is swallowed by the mini-Sun.

A few minutes later, her instruments concur with what everybody's eyes surely see. The mini-Sun starts burning brighter. *Is this why they do it?* Na-Yeli can't help but wonder. *But such a process can never be self-sustainable ...*

*T*hese dead and mortally wounded animals are sacrificed to the mini-Sun, Na-Yeli thinks, *and the whole ritual is so perfectly timed that either they've rehearsed–and practiced–this to death, or they have some form of silent, mutual communication.* A multi-species hive mind? Something, someone must have told them or taught them to do this. A sacrifice ritual so crazy, yet so complex must have some extremely interesting background.

It's grist to the Slow CEO's mill–mulling over a multitude of data, making sense of the whole. The helicopter point-of-view, even as the helicopter mind fails to see the inherent sustainability of the process.

Suppose the sacrificed animals provide fuel for this mini-Sun, her thinking goes, *then this is the most stupefying example of an Ouroboros Gaia possible.* The consumed animals feed the mini-Sun, the mini-Sun beams energy down for the photosynthesis of the plants and trees, the megafauna's prey eats the flora, the megafauna eats the prey, and part of the megafauna is sacrificed. None of these processes is one hundred percent efficient, far from it. So lots of energy gets wasted in the process. Then why does the cycle keep going? It should have stopped dead in its tracks, starved for energy, long ago.

There's something she's missing, and utterly fascinated that she now is, she intends to get to the bottom of this. She's so captivated that she forgets to move with caution, making as little sound as possible. She doesn't notice that she might be noticed.

While reluctantly heading north–deep inside, Na-Yeli wishes to solve this layer's conundrums before moving onwards to the next–through the dense vegetation in the tropical heat of the foliage's viridescent reflection, Na-Yeli and the Moiety Alien chance upon a large clearing. This one doesn't seem tailor-made for some arcane, far-fetched ritual–it looks like a natural glade. It's also quite big. They could save time by crossing it, but they need to be cautious.

Standing still for a few minutes, while carefully scanning the surroundings for megafauna, Na-Yeli and her instruments call it safe. She moves into the clearing and the Moiety Alien follows. When they're almost at the middle of it, Na-Yeli hears a giant 'swoosh' followed by the massive clap of two half-bowls of reddish wood slamming together at the rims, capturing the Moiety Alien in the process. The two wooden half-bowls–has the force of the clap glued the two halves together, Na-Yeli wonders in disbelief–become an encapsulating globe as four Stomposaurs rush into the clearing, surrounding Na-Yeli before she can run away. Her alien exterior doesn't seem to faze them, quite probably they're not the first aliens being caught.

She doesn't fight. These animals are so big, she doesn't know how, let alone where to start. One of them could stamp her to six feet below with one of its humongous hoofs. Now that she thinks of it, even for such super-sized animals their feet–hoofs, paws, whatever–are quite big relative to their body size. A sign of divergent evolution? In any case, she surrenders or hopes that raising her hands is interpreted as such, and hopes to come with an escape plan, later. Especially after this eerily coordinated megafauna ambush that captured the Moiety Alien in its globular prison.

Without further ado, they lead Na-Yeli–and roll the wooden globe containing the Moiety Alien– towards the rectangular sacrificial site, next to the colossal trebuchet tree. On its far edge, under the shadow of the gigantic catapult tree, lies a big net. Na-Yeli is driven onto the net, the wooden contraption containing her alien partner is rolled right next to her, and then the net is hoisted ten or so meters in the air. *An impromptu prison until the time is right for the next sacrifice*, Na-Yeli thinks.

She waits until it's dark and the Ultragiraffes guarding her are becoming sleepy. Then she drills, as surreptitiously and silently as she can, a small hole in the wooden wall of the Moiety Alien's prison. Once she's through, she shines a light in. She waits and soon, through her infrared camera, sees part of the Moiety Alien extend itself through the small hole. *It doesn't need much*, she thinks and then gestures it to go back. It seems to understand her–their silent interactions as they traversed through this weird layer greatly improved their gesticulative/movement vocabulary–and moves back in its, now breached, prison.

Na-Yeli and the Moiety Alien could make a run for it, but since the megafauna knows they're here, they'd only get the biggest posse of this weird world hunting for them. No, she's thinking of a different plan–escape in plain sight, as it were–that will also get them closer to one of the big mysteries ruling this layer. For the other big mystery in this layer, she intends to get help from a very close friend. On top of that, right here is the best place to have an undisturbed sleep in this whole Mesozoic Park gone wild.

W hen Na-Yeli wakes up the next morning, she can still feel the aftermath of the migraine that a LateralSys possession brings with it. *Must have been quite a session*, Na-Yeli–the Slow CEO –thinks as day breaks and several Über-Gorillas are already schlepping the massive leather pouch in position. Overnight, Na-Yeli's nanomachines have harvested more useful materials from both her encapsulating net and the Moiety Alien's wooden prison. She now has sufficient material to form viable wings in this air and gravity. She only needs to get out just in time. She likes the Icarus legend, she doesn't want to be its female–and alien– incarnation.

As the preparations for the big ritual proceed through the dawn–Na-Yeli reckons that captured aliens are entitled to their own ritual–she reads through LateralSys's findings.

That was quite a challenge you left for me, sister, and my special thanks for this, as such *almost* indecipherable mysteries are the intellectual grist to my mind's mill. Megafauna that understand each other without an obvious means of communication? Telepathy is the first thing that comes to mind. Not very scientific at first sight, mind you, but if it looks like a duck, walks like a duck, and quacks like a duck ...

On an oblique whim, I modified some of the crystals you sampled from the Fractal Maze into highly sensitive echo chambers. I had to stretch my makeshift instruments to the limit. I had to scan a huge swath of the frequency spectrum before I got a faint response.

Something's going on, but it happens at a level that's barely above the measuring threshold. The best I can call it is a superposed enabler. Remember AM and FM radio, where our predecessors would vary the amplitude or frequency of a radio wave so that it could be encoded for sound & music? Take it a step further and we get how certain crystals, when vibrating, can superpose a huge range of frequencies on an AC carrier wave, used for condition monitoring back in the days.

Now imagine the logical end result of that; i.e. an adaptive, very weak—hence almost impossible to detect—electromagnetic pattern that is yet complex enough to exhibit self-replication, self-sentience, the will to survive, and propagation through symbiosis.

In somewhat the same way that our DNA reacts to its environment and sets up a species—not individuals—for survival in the long run through adaptations. In that way ensuring its own survival in the long run. Thing is, it may change *itself*—change is one of the two constants—while keeping its basic structure—the second constant—intact. That is, the content of our DNA—the way the A-, T-, G-, and C-bases are encoded—changes, while its basic structure—the double helix—remains the same. Selfish genes, indeed.

I suspect these superposed patterners use the same trick. While the actual content—the amount of amplitude and frequency modulation—changes, the way it's structured—the carrier waves in the host—remains the same.

They also need to adapt the megafauna to new circumstances for their host's species—not the individual animals—to survive, but since circumstances in these layers change much faster than they do on a planet, they need to adapt much faster.

So I strongly suspect that these emergent electromagnetic patterns somehow evolved a megafauna hive mind that tries to keep the environment the same. The larger picture seems simple—if the mini-Sun does, they die. From our instruments, I noticed that the output of the mini-Sun did increase after it assimilated the sacrifice. Hence, when it's running out of fuel, so to speak, it will dim. The megafauna and their, well, electromagnetic parasites or symbionts—take your pick—notice, as well, and decide to do something about it.

I extensively checked the footage our cameras made of the megafauna and did find that some of the Über-Gorillas have catapults. So either they already invented the catapult and the communal hive mind decided to manufacture a stupendously large one, even if that doesn't explain the happy coincidence of a single, super-large tree with just the right form.

That's when I made my second find—the trees are infested with it, too. The Ultragiraffes mainly function as antenna towers in treeless places like large clearings and the savannah outside the equatorial tropical jungle. Otherwise, the trees keep the hive mind together.

This might explain why they simply don't catapult dead flora into the mini-Sun, as my calculations hint that every little bit needs to be recycled to keep this ecosystem viable. Only the most difficult to recycle materials—dead megafauna, especially those that have had a long life—can be sacrificed to keep the mini-Sun going. And quite probably the communal hive mind somehow self-selected for the growth of a singular, even-oversized-in-their-world, trebuchet tree.

There's a huge pattern there—controlled by a minuscule one—but still, the pieces don't quite fit. There's no way that burning dead animals brings back sufficient energy to keep this whole crazy ecosystem going. There must be other sources of energy that maintain this ecosystem.

So do keep KillBitch handy in our sojourn to the mini-Sun, as she is much faster than you (or I). No offense intended, I just want to live to tell —and experience—this tale.

Finally, I have a shocker for you, baby. Most of the measuring results I got were from the nearby Ultragiraffes, who are natural amplifiers and antennas, and the trebuchet tree—once I realized they were in it, too—from which we're hanging. The only other ones from the odd, sleepless Zeppelinfant and Stomposaur who were sniffing at you, thinking you were asleep (in a way, they were right), and then got into range of my makeshift equipment. The megafauna, most probably, has developed a special sensitivity for the signals, so they even sense it over a few tens of meters. The trees are key, and the Ultragiraffe's neck antennas carry the signals over a wider range, establishing the megafauna hive mind on open plains.

But then I accidentally turned the measuring equipment on myself, and lo and behold, there was a response. These emergent patterns, this superposed intelligence, whatever you like to call it: we're infected with it, as well.

Once we have some time, I urge you to look into this.

–LateralSys;

*W*ell, that's indeed an answer to the existence of the megafauna's hive mind, Na-Yeli, ever the Slow CEO, can't help but think, *but it doesn't explain where these 'superposed aliens' themselves come from.* Something to worry about later, as the preparations for the ritual continue.

Na-Yeli and the wooden contraption encapsulating the Moiety Alien are lowered from the trebuchet tree. Na-Yeli is driven, and the Moiety Alien is rolled onto the giant leather pouch. Na-Yeli doesn't resist, and neither do the Über-Gorillas guiding her seem surprised that she doesn't try to make a run for it as if accepting to be the–literal–sacrificial goat is the most natural thing in the world.

Staying cool and quite happy that nobody noticed the little escape hole she drilled in the Moiety Alien's prison, Na-Yeli takes her place, right next to the Moiety Alien, on the launching seat. The long ropes from the trebuchet tree are tied to the big square leather receptacle and the launching animals appear in the square clearing as the mini-Sun rises in a partly cloudy sky.

A communal meal is eaten at high noon. For this special event, hunter, and prey, carnivore, omnivore and herbivore delve into pre-prepared food while ignoring each other's hunt-and-flee instincts. Then, to Na-Yeli's bafflement, they perform stretching exercises and sparring rituals in preparation for the all-important launch. They didn't do this at the previous ritual, so is this special? Because now they're sacrificing aliens?

As the mini-Sun is slowly moving to the West, the multitude of animals bite, grip, or otherwise get hold of the many leather strips connected to the giant leather pouch. They're waiting for the sign–a sign Na-Yeli isn't attuned to hear–as the tension mounts in a deafening silence.

The sacrifice hymn, haunting and exhilarating, rears its melodic head. *It wasn't just the wounded, sacrificial animals singing it*, Na-Yeli now realizes, *it was all of them*. Looking at the branches and leaves of the nearby trees, swaying and vibrating in tune with the poignant theme, it seems to trees are partaking, in their own way, as well.

Step by step, the animals are moving back. The ropes are stretched tight and the two branches of the tallest tree in this mini-world are bent back, bit by bit. Na-Yeli leans back in the pouch, and signals for the Moiety Alien to come out at her signal. Belatedly, she hopes it–and she–will be able to take the sudden acceleration. But if they've both been carefully selected for this trip–and she certainly was–then this should be something they should be able to endure.

The evocative hymns rise in time with the slow stretching of the super-sized slingshot, an elegiac tune as taut as the long ropes from the trebuchet tree. A tension in the air like the sudden humidity in the atmosphere before the onset of thunder. The song accelerating like Peer Gynt's "In the Hall of the Mountain King" on acid–savage like an upstaged avatar–mixed with Carl Orff's "O Fortuna" and powered by the guitars from Hell. Megafauna muscles vibrate with stress, ropes and thick leather are strained with tension, the air is filled with a taunting crescendo. Something's got to give.

Then, as the fever pitch is reached and both the trebuchet tree's main branches almost appear to snap, the myriad of animals let go as one and Na-Yeli and the Moiety Alien–who shrunk/expanded itself out of its wooden prison a sparse second before the launch–are whiplashed into the sky.

The intensity of the event has etched itself deep into Na-Yeli's soul and the snap and the massive acceleration of the launch push her over the edge of pain and oblivion. As the Slow CEO faints, KillBitch rises to the fore, utterly animated, bellowing a primal scream. *Top this, Bitches!*

No time to enjoy the ride, she has to act blindingly fast. As they are released from the leather launching pouch and the acceleration dwindles, she shape-shifts into a more aerodynamic shape, gesturing for the Moiety Alien to stay behind her back. Then she soars, air under her wings and sharply turns to the left, barely missing the mini-Sun, its intense radiation burning on her–radiation-shielded–belly. Nobody morphs as fast and furious –and effectively–as KillBitch.

Getting a real close-up view, KillBitch–and her instruments–now see that the mini-Sun is actually scraping the sky; that is the small sun is rolling along the upper barrier of the layer, like a spherical chariot of fire riding along the curve of the sky.

The Slow CEO would then understand that the mini-Sun's heat is not just from chemical fire, but also from the spaghettification of its outer layer as it touches the impenetrable, forbidding barrier. Molecules are spaghettified to their atomic constituents and rain down–invisibly–from the sky. Ashes to atomic ashes, dust to disintegrated dust. This looks more and more like a closed system–Na-Yeli would muse, later, but KillBitch is only preoccupied with survival.

So she makes a few close turns around the mini-Sun–taking care to stay clear of the barrier, as she does remember the close encounter she had with it in the previous layers–to take a few extra recordings, just because she can. Then she gets overconfident and gets too close to the mini-Sun with one of her wings, just as a mini-solar flare erupts from it. Some of the metamaterials catch fire and an overpowering plasma pulse shoots through the control wires, destroying them.

KillBitch loses control of her right wing and is now circling down in an accelerating spiral. If KillBitch had any knowledge of Icarus, the legend would have said 'I told you so' to her. Now she's just going down, faster and faster, cursing all the way.

Somehow the Moiety Alien gets under her and breaks her fall, somewhat. Not quite enough as she keeps going in her downward spiral, but now the speed feels survivable. They crash—why the Moiety Alien stays with her even through that is something also KillBitch doesn't get—with KillBitch's non-functioning wing and its very sharp edges pointing downwards. The wing stays rigid as the air is filled with a big rip and KillBitch and the Moiety Alien don't crash land on the forest floor, but rather crash almost right through it, into a crackling, flickering light show below ...

Ultimately, Na-Yeli's fall through the forest floor—which isn't quite as thick as she would've thought, hence the megafauna's oversized feet—is broken because her outstretched, heavily damaged right wing bumps into ... something. After the fall was broken, and there was no imminent, life-threatening situation, her adrenalin wore off, KillBitch retreated and Na-Yeli—the Slow CEO—returned. As all the artificial nerves of her right wing have burned out when it touched the mini-Sun, Na-Yeli feels nothing except a minor vibration.

Because KillBitch has retreated, Na-Yeli assumes she's back in safe waters and has time to mull things over. So much new information, so many fresh avenues to explore. But the smell of something burning brings her to her senses, as that something burning may very well be ... her right wing.

Stuck halfway through the undergrowth, hanging in the balance as it were, she aims some of her cameras at her right wing's end, only to see that it's touching the lower barrier of this layer, the metamaterials of her wing's exoskin spaghettifying away. She morphs claws on her functioning left wing and feet, gets a firm grip on the forest floor, and slowly pulls herself up and away from the lower barrier that's barely two meters below the undergrowth.

I should not make a habit of this, Na-Yeli thinks, *getting addicted to spaghettification might make me the stupidest junkie, ever*. But if the inner barrier is so close, something else might be going on. Na-Yeli sends in a few Kittis to see exactly what. The things they see are enlightening.

Matter from the forest floor keeps falling onto the inner barrier, spaghettifying into its atomic constituents. Through the developed heat and radiation these atoms rise up and are re-absorbed by the giant trees, who seem to have developed a sort of reverse-root-cum-photosynthesis system. *As above, so below*, Na-Yeli muses, *this fills in the large gap in the ecosystem's energy budget*. Then add the odd, captured alien–shot into the mini-Sun, if it's unlucky–and this Berserker Forest has some extra matter to maintain its mad equilibrium.

At some point in the future, the evolutionary paths of the mega-flora and -fauna's DNA and their superposed partners might diverge, and then it'll be interesting to see who might prevail. But Na-Yeli has bigger fish to fry and can't hang around to find out. While the Slow CEO is fascinated by life in this layer, she also has more pressing matters at hand.

Such as fixing the now mostly dead appendage that is her right wing. Like getting extra materials while the getting is good–the undergrowth is rich in minerals, rare metals, and other volatiles–like getting away before the megafauna starts hunting for them, and tries to shoot them into their mini-Sun, again.

But before Na-Yeli can shape-shift her exoskin into a more bipedal form and haul her alien partner to make a run for it, she looks up to see that she and the Moiety Alien are surrounded by the megafauna. *Oh well*, Na-Yeli thinks, *this time I'm not gonna wait through the night, but make our escape well before that.* She rolls her eyes. *Just watch this bitch climb to the very top of your trebuchet tree, and then jump off it as she shape-shifts into a glider, up, up, and away to the North Pole.*

Then she notices the way the Ultragiraffes, Zeppelinfants, Stomposaurs, Über-Gorillas, and other megafauna watch her and the Moiety Alien. Not like hunters chasing prey. Not like guardians happy to re-catch their quarry. But with a look of ... respect? Maybe even ... awe?

Before settling down for the night near the polar circle, Na-Yeli gets down from one of the Stomposaurs that accompany her and the Moiety Alien and starts to unfold the two huge woolen blankets–or at least the closest thing, using mainly local hemp–that she'd prepared. Or, more exactly, that she programmed the large array of mini-bots to convert from the hemp plants they gathered along the way. With the help of the Moiety Alien–how it is able to hold on to one side of the blanket is beyond her–they cover the shivering animals that normally never venture beyond the tropics. The Stomposaurs, feeling that their temperatures rise back to normal levels, nod their heads in appreciation–a gesture they copied from Na-Yeli and the Moiety Alien.

After Na-Yeli has fed the huge carnivores with the preserved meat of a few herbivores, she prepares her own broth, which now has some carefully sterilized, yet fresh ingredients from the

Berserker Forest. She'll get back to the hyper-recycled stuff when she has to. As the mini-Sun sets, they go to sleep, as they have a lot of work to do, tomorrow. Na-Yeli's sleep is fitful, and undisturbed by the ghosts of the past. Her stocks are fully replenished, her batteries fully charged, and she will be as well-rested as she'll ever be. Dog knows what awaits them in the next layer.

But first, they have to get to the Diaphragm Gate. As she reminisced about events just before she went asleep, Na-Yeli had a little inkling. The megafauna has large feet to avoid falling through the undergrowth towards the inner barrier. It's also why they can walk so silently. But these large, uncovered feet will get terribly cold on the North Pole's ice. So she reprogrammed her mini-bots–she hadn't recycled them yet–to convert the remainder of the hemp (thank dog she brought too much of it, as these Stomposaurs can carry a lot) into eight large, thickly insulated shoes.

It takes her a while to show her intention with the shoes to the Stomposaurs. They finally get the gist of it as she gestures them–and her wish is almost like a command to them–to put their large snouts in the permafrost, feeling the cold. Then repeat it with a shoe covering their snout. As a kind of understanding dawns on them, they let her put on the shoes, one by one.

Then she demonstrates how they can take them off–they'll need to, once they return to the tropics– and finally, they can be on their way. Yet Na-Yeli doesn't mind the delay, she's quite enjoying herself in the Berserker Forest layer. However, duty beckons and they head for the North Pole.

Having arrived at the very North Pole itself, Na-Yeli triple-checks the coordinates of her instruments and then marks the exact position of North on the ice. Then she lowers the makeshift jackhammer she manufactured before they left, carried by the other Stomposaur. Luckily, the ice is only about thirty meters thick here–she measured the distance to the outer barrier with her lidar and radar just before they arrived–so it shouldn't take their giant companions that much works to pierce through it. First, Na-Yeli uses a telescopic torch to anchor the central pin as deep in the ice as possible. Then she connects the circular jackhammer and ties the two Stomposaurs to it while making sure they have the silencers she's prepared in their ears, as the jackhammer will be loud. At her command, they begin walking a circle, chasing each other's backs.

The hacksaw-cum-ratchet mechanism she designed is now cutting a large circle in the ice. It can only go a few meters deep, so when it has gone as far as it can go, she disconnects the Stomposaurs, takes out the equipment, and lowers some home-made TNT in the central bore and a few choice other positions, where she drills small holes with her torch. Then she leads the Stomposaurs and the Moiety Alien a safe distance away from the very North Pole, gestures the Stomposaurs to sit down. She waits until the Stomposaurs have lowered themselves on their haunches, sets the silencers in their ears to a higher setting, then detonates the TNT.

Jolted by the explosion, the Stomposaurs quickly get up, but by then Na-Yeli makes shushing sounds–which they probably don't hear, but she can't help herself–and calming gestures. Incredibly, they overrule their fleeing instinct and don't run away. After they've sufficiently cooled down, Na-Yeli leads them to the–now somewhat lower–North Pole again, and sets up the cutting equipment for a somewhat smaller circle, in this way preparing a step-terraced construction that makes ascending–and descending–easier for both her and the Stomposaurs.

After repeating the procedure five times, at a depth of about twenty-nine meters, the unmistakable circle of light of the transitional portal becomes visible through the transparent ice.

Na-Yeli uses some more of her home-made TNT to blow it free—no chance she'll blast through the lower barrier nor through the mysteriously selectively permeable membrane—and prepares a few Kittis (she even had time to clone a few new ones to replace the ones that went missing when entering the 'Sea of Hyperwaves' layer) to check out the other side.

She sends them in, programmed to report back after ten minutes. In the meantime, she leads the Stomposaurs out of the ice mine they've created, uses all possible gestures and sounds she can think of to express how thankful she is—these creatures are just way too big to be hugged—and bids them goodbye. Does she imagine it, or are the Stomposaurs reluctant to leave? And is there a certain amount of kindness, maybe even affection in their expressions?

After their return from the mini-Sun, the collective mind of the megaflora and megafauna completely changed its attitude towards Na-Yeli and the Moiety Alien. As if they've passed some divine test—thank dog they never surmised that falling from the sky like a modern-day Icarus was definitely not her intention—they were treated like gods or at least chariots of the gods.

They were proffered food, a few Über-Gorillas offered to help with Na-Yeli's malfunctioning right wing and the rest of the animals made it abundantly clear that they were willing to help the two of them in any way possible. An offer she couldn't refuse, eventually deciding to take the two biggest Stomposaurs with them to help them drill through the North Pole's ice.

It's with a leaden heart that Na-Yeli sees the Stomposaurs recede in the distance, still wearing her oversized faux woollies and shoes. Her intense fascination with this layer–she baptized it 'The Berserker Forest'–has turned into a deep appreciation. She's come to love this place and would have dearly loved to stay longer, but she must continue with the mission.

DOOM BELLS

through the noise it takes a while to see-ee eeh-he
doom bells are ringing for you and me-ee eeh-he

She never thought she'd regret leaving a layer, but there she is. Two more layers–at least, if the spacing between them remains approximately the same–to go before they hit the Core, with unknown dangers–and opportunities–ahead, but still she wishes they–the Moiety Alien has become a faithful companion– could have stayed a bit longer. In any case, she's replenished her stocks as much as possible and is as ready to enter the next stage as ever.

First, she must explore the next layer with a couple of probes, to see how perilous–or safe–it is, and, if necessary, to make preparations. While she sends five of her Kittis through the semi-permeable membrane, the Moiety Alien approaches it as well, four of its orbitals pointing to the Diaphragm Gate. Then the orbitals right in front of the gate shrink to near-nothingness as the other four double in size. It's almost impossible to see, but Na-Yeli gets the very strong impression that the Moiety Alien 'dips' its minimized orbitals through the diaphragm. Then its biggest orbitals shrink, very quickly, and get back to their maximum size just as quickly.

The Moiety Alien jumps back as if it's experienced something scary, painful, or both. *Interesting,* Na-Yeli thinks, *is that how it knew that it couldn't go through the gate at the bottom of the sea in layer three?*

In the meantime, after their allotted ten minutes have expired, all of her five Kittis come back, but not quite in one piece. Their semi-sentience could best be described as dazed and confused, and while most of their instruments still function fine, a few have been ruptured.

The atmosphere on the other side is almost Earth-normal, with 89% N_2, 10% O_2, and several traces of noble gases. An unusually high amount of metal particles–in particular Cu, Ni, Al, and Si– while the pressure, when they were still able to measure it, is 1.03 bar and the temperature is a sweltering 313 $^{\circ}$K–hot, but nothing her cooling system can't handle. Which wouldn't seem so bad, were it not for the fact that all the probe's microphones and sensitive pressure transmitters have been utterly destroyed.

Before they gave up the ghost, the probes' microphones measured excessive sound pressures in the frequency range of 300 to 4600 Hz. Sound pressures upwards of 180 decibels. Which doesn't sound that extreme until Na-Yeli finds, through a quick database check, that decibel follows a logarithmic scale. In other words, 100dB is loud– the sound of a jackhammer like the one they had to use to get through the ice at the Berserker Forest's North Pole–130 dB–the pain threshold of human hearing–is one thousand times as loud, and 180 decibel is *one hundred thousand* times as loud as that. It's a sound pressure almost beyond belief, very close to–she checks her database again–the maximum possible sound pressure in air with a pressure of one bar, which is 194 dB. If the sound pressure gets any higher the fluctuations in air pressure it creates become so large that the low-pressure region hits zero pressure–a vacuum–and it's physically impossible to go lower than that.

In any case, these are sound levels that will not just rupture her eardrums but will wreak havoc with her internal organs, as well. And she doesn't want to contemplate what they would do to the orbitals of her friend, the Moiety Alien. They can't go in there unprepared, they have to take some kind of precaution. Make that several kinds of precautions.

Na-Yeli thanks the fates that they have been able to carry a surplus of materials from the Berserker Forest–where they eventually were treated like gods–and sets out protective measures. For one, the excessively loud sound can be dampened, but the sound levels they seem to be up against are so extreme that they would need some twenty meters or so of sound-isolating material, which they don't have, let alone will be able to transport through the Diaphragm Gate.

Sound can be canceled out by anti-sound, which is the same sound but with the opposite phase. There are two problems–OK, let's call them challenges–with that. First, she needs to know the frequencies that carry the dangerous sound levels. For that, she can send scouting probes–carefully insulated, and with extremely sturdy microphones –in front of them, to measure the exact sound before it hits them. *Better make a huge amount of these*, Na-Yeli thinks, *as they can be the sacrificial fodder that saves our asses*.

Second, to fully cancel the amplitude of the dangerous sound, they need to transmit an equal amplitude at the opposite phase. 180 decibels–or even the theoretical limit of 194 decibels, let's assume the worst–contains a tremendous amount of energy. To fully cancel that, her anti-speakers need to be huge and stupendously powerful. While she could conceivably prepare a pair of such ultraspeakers, she simply doesn't have enough energy to keep them going throughout the half-round trip to the next Diaphragm Gate.

It's not the pressure difference of the 194 dB sound waves that's the problem: these are merely about 2 bar (from zero bar at the bottom end to 2 bar at the top end). No, it's the energy they carry: at 194 dB that's more than 10 MegaWatt per square meter. She needs to dampen that with the same amount of energy to make the resulting sound waves bearable.

But where does she get the energy from? She needs a pocket-sized nuclear reactor to generate this amount of energy, and she simply doesn't have it. But then she remembers her early judo lessons: "use the force of your opponent against him." Yes, it's as if KillBitch and LateralSys are giving her hints at the same time.

She must absorb the power of the incoming sound waves and then immediately send it back to them transformed as anti-sound. While the principle is sound (pun unintended), she must keep a dynamic balance, walk a dancing tightrope; that is, if she makes the canceling out too effective, she will not receive enough incoming energy for the next upcoming blast of noise. If she makes the canceling not effective enough, the leaked sounds will kill or severely hurt her and her friends.

This may tax my onboard computer to the max, Na-Yeli thinks, *only one way to find out.* So there she is, designing–with all the engineering data of humanity's history backed up in her triple-redundant quantum computers to help her–a type of metamaterial that not only can reflect tremendous amounts of energy but at exactly the right frequencies, as well.

Luckily, predecessors of it have been made in huge quantities, often at high-quality levels. They were called loudspeakers. And what Na-Yeli is producing is derived from the good old electrostatic loudspeaker (ESL), with the biggest difference being the power source.

While this energy-absorption-and-reflecting-energy-back will never be 100% efficient, that's fine, as she intends to use the surplus energy for propulsion (judo trick part two).

The membrane of metamaterials she's designing must both constantly absorb the energy aimed at her and reflect it as anti-sound. That's her next problem–they never seem to end–as she can't do both at the same time. And letting one membrane absorb while another reflects also doesn't work because they're in each other's way.

Well, what about the principle of Alternating Current, Na-Yeli thinks, *applied to this crazy acoustic set-up*. Assuming 50 Hertz, that would be 20 milliseconds of absorption alternated with 20 milliseconds of reflection. And she can increase or decrease the frequency to see what works best. But that would still leak a lot of the incoming power. Thus, below membrane 1 we have membrane 2: reflecting the leaking power at itself using the same principle. Followed by membrane 3, etcetera. Membranes all the way down? No, at some point the leaked-through noise should be bearable. On top of that, she intends to use as much of the absorbed power for propulsion as she can get away with.

She can almost hear her triple-redundant quantum computer crunch (or should it beep?) as it performs the necessary calculations. Four membranes should do the trick, yet she has enough material for five. So five it'll be.

But if those membranes rupture–especially the outer ones at the stupendous sound pressures they must produce–enough high dB noise can leak in that can either kill or seriously wound her or the Moiety Alien. So she'd better prepare an army of nano-repair bots in between all these layers to constantly repair cracks and ruptures. Well, at least they'll have enough sound energy to vibration-weld with.

Finally, the triple electrostatic loudspeaker membrane (ELM) shield has to be flexible, so that– for example–she can dive in first into this hypersound inferno with the forward half of the enveloping ELM shield around her, followed by the Moiety Alien in the other half. And vice-versa if– hopefully when–they can exit this insane layer.

And sound waves also disperse in air. So could she run away from them? Two problems with that– the speed of sound in air, and the amount of dispersion. The sound waves will come at her at Mach 1, or one thousand and two hundred and twenty-four kilometers per hour. She just can't fly that fast. And the dispersion at the maximum possible pressure is too slow. Records of the Krakatau explosion in 1883 measured 172 decibels at 160 kilometers from the erupting volcano (assuming it produced the full 194 dB at its very center). That covers about 90% of this layer.

So she can't run and she can't hide. She and her alien companion must face the tremendous sound waves head-on and hope their ELM shield works and keeps working.

Then the next, possible disastrous notion, strikes her. The thickness of each layer, so far, is 13.75 kilometers (at some point this regularity must break down, or the Core is only 8 kilometers across). To the best of her knowledge, the barriers between the layers are impenetrable to sound, as well. So they can act as echo chambers, meaning that the wavefront of sound that she has just successfully passed through might be reflected at her–even if at a somewhat lower sound pressure–a bit later on. Or not just at her back, but from her sides, and from above and below. From basically any direction. Even without reverberations, the sound wave would complete a full round trip–say 151 km on average–about every 7 minutes and then would have a dispersion of about 15 dB per round trip.

Holy smokes, Na-Yeli quickly calculates, *six times of being hit with the same sound wave–every 7 minutes–before it dampens below the pain threshold.* And that without taking into account the reverberations of that stupendous sound wave against the globular barriers of this penultimate layer.

On the sunny side, that same sound wave should clash with itself, and reflections of itself, which would be mostly out of phase with each other. It'll be a myriad of sound waves, the original mixing with itself and its echoes until it finally disperses and smothers itself–even while occasionally re-amplifying parts of itself back to 194 dB (as higher is impossible). On average forty-two minutes before the original sound wave has dampened below the pain threshold of 130 dB.

In any case, she does not only need scouting probes in front of her, she needs to be enveloped in a cloud of probes. Even as sturdy as she can make them, some will still fail, so she needs plenty for backup. In a flash of foresight, she'd cloned a lot of Kittis on their route to the North Pole in the Berserker Forest layer, figuring she should do that while she had the time and opportunity. Now she's glad as she can use them all for her Soundcloud of Kittis as pre-detectors, all attached to the forward part of her ELM shield in order to get all that non-biological matter through the semi-permeable membrane.

They're almost ready to dive in—she explained her findings and plans to the best of her ability to the Moiety Alien—but she wants to perform a few more measurements first. She sends in her modified, much sturdier Kittis in ten-minute in-and-out explorations in order to pinpoint the source of the massive sound waves. Where it is if there's more than one source and if it—or they—are moving towards the Diaphragm Gate. If only to prevent them from going in when the very source of this auditory horror is straight upon them.

Over one hour, her Kittis not only survive but pinpoint no less than three possible sources of the sound waves. Only one of these appears to be in 'line of sight'–better make that 'line of sound', Na-Yeli thinks–and two seem to be beyond the horizon of the inner globular barrier. It doesn't tell her much, only that the chances of it appearing on their doorstep, as it were, are very small. Her systems are ready, she gestures to the Moiety Alien, which gives its assent, and in they go, Kittis first, then Na-Yeli and the forward half of the ELM shield followed by the Moiety Alien in the aft half. The ELM shield feed-forwarded by the Kitti Soundcloud.

Na-Yeli holds her breath–both mentally and physically–as the first, wildly fluctuating sound leaks hit her. It hurts like hell for the first few seconds while the system adapts, shifts frequencies, and improves the anti-sound reflections. She eyes the Moiety Alien, who shows no signs of distress. Probably because she braced herself, the pain is not too horrible.

Next, she gradually transforms the ELM shield which is now effectively their metamaterial exoskin into something resembling a hang-glider, as gliding is still the most energy-efficient mode of transport in an atmosphere. This disturbs the efficiency of the ELM shield so she must perform this shape-shifting maneuver with care, slower than she normally performs it, slower than she'd like. But she has no choice.

Finally, they're ready to go—Na-Yeli on top of the Moiety Alien as this seems to be the best way to leverage most of its mysterious floatation power—looking like a cross between a hang-glider and the classic Jumbo 747. Na-Yeli checks her system's last reckoning of the origin of the last massive sound wave, and then, on a hunch, plots a course not the furthest away from it, but relatively close by.

It's not quite fly-by-wire, as Na-Yeli remains firmly in control, but rather survive-by-wire as they will not last long if the ELM shield fails. Yet she still manages to get their shape aerodynamically optimized for extra lift. She's going to need it, as the gravity in this layer averages 0.78 G and the pressure close to Earth normal, meaning it's getting close to the edge of conditions where she can still hang-glide. As such, this whole contraption is her personal sound castle in the sky.

The processing power of her triple-redundant quantum computers is stretched to the limit as the massive amount of vibration data comes in through three dimensions. Exacting extrapolations, intricate interpolations, constantly evolving inferences—the system crunches numbers to save its life. Literally.

The ELM shield provides both Na-Yeli and the Moiety Alien with a protective, three-dimensional wave of sound cancellation (and some extra thrust, to boot). The fact that both of them are still alive proofs that the system is working. Gradually, Na-Yeli diverts more energy to her ion thruster, speeding them up. The noise that does pass through is loud, multitudinous, irritating, and distracting, but bearable. It's frightening, haunting, yet eerily familiar.

Then it strikes Na-Yeli. *It sounds like a church bell*, she thinks, *way out of tune, with a thousand overtones and reverberations, but the first wave–the original–is like a bell*. She pays more attention to it. *Unmistakably*.

Closer to the Core, they don't have that much distance to travel from opening to opening–if circumstances allow them to take the shortest route –so Na-Yeli and the Moiety Alien should reach the final opening in less than ninety minutes if nothing holds them up.

Only then does it occur to her to check her cameras. She's been so focused on sound–basically on how to survive in this sonic inferno–that she merely expected nothing but darkness. She's wrong. The sky is alive with colors, a mesmerizing kaleidoscope of ghostly appearances, a mix of constant lightning–with certainly no lack of thunder–and Aurorae Borealis.

Crazy, multihued apparitions, sometimes branched like lightning, sometimes curtained like polar light, sometimes self-similar like fractals. *Sonoluminescence lighting up the sky*, Na-Yeli thinks, *whiplashed so hard by sheer noise it glows in response.* Not sure if it's the N_2 or O_2 that's occasionally lighting up or the many, many metal particles that saturate this atmosphere, but the end result sure is pretty, and awe-inspiring. The things she can show her family and friends if she survives all this.

Her radar and lidar–her sonar is useless in this extremely noisy environment–warn her of an incoming object. Thankfully, it's not coming directly at them but is merely passing inside the radar's range. It's moving at about 40 kilometers per hour–something they can easily dodge. Na-Yeli combines the measurements of both sonar and lidar to get an appropriate size of the object. The numbers are crunched and the first estimate rolls out and Na-Yeli gasps. *A globular object of sixty-five meters across*, she thinks, *and I have a very strong inkling of what it's made of.*

She checks the frequency response spectrum of the first and most powerful sound wave and compares it with a few from her database. Spectra from way back, when expert craftsman created a mold, then carefully cast and ground a bronze mass into a well-sounding bell.

The data don't match exactly, but for all intents and purposes, it's close enough. Characteristic peaks in the 360 to 4800 Hertz range, and while the intensity of her measurements is right at the very top of the scale, the shapes are remarkably similar. *I'm willing to bet good money that this 65-meter monstrosity bouncing around here is made mainly of bronze*, Na-Yeli thinks, *which would put its weight at about a thousand tons*. A bell from Hell. A Doom Bell.

The momentum of such a cannonball is immense. At some point, this almost unstoppable force meets a truly unmovable object—one of the two barriers of this layer. Why it's such an unyielding barrier is something Na-Yeli hopes to find out, even if right now she's at a loss. In any case, this massive bronze ball bounces against this unbreakable wall at 40 kps, rings like a bell, releasing something in the order of 150 Megajoules of energy, causing sound waves that would do the Krakatau eruption proud.

Now that she's got the course and speed of the object, Na-Yeli and her equipment can extrapolate where it will bounce off the barrier again and know where the first—and loudest—sound wave will come from. This should greatly reduce the computational stress of her anti-sound system, the one thing for which she has no backup. But the calculations don't add up to the massive cacophony they're experiencing.

Don't tell me there's more than one, Na-Yeli, forced to think the unthinkable. So she calculates for two, for three, for four. Three bells match their measured monster sounds best. As if on cue, her radar and lidar report a second globular object, this time 64 meters across, moving at about the same speed. *The little brother*, Na-Yeli thinks, *for your value of 'little', as it will release only some 143 MegaJoules per bounce.* Ten minutes later, the third one comes into view—the first one having already disappeared beyond the horizon—clicking in at 66 meters, with about the same speed, releasing about 157 MJ/bounce.

Since it knows what is causing these maxed-out sound waves, her system becomes more predictive. It knows the approximate size, last position, and momentum of the three objects—and by correlating all the incoming data from their sound-and-vision sensor cloud these approximations become ever more precise—and it knows the size and exact borders of this penultimate layer. So it can predict where the next bounces of these bronze billiard balls against the round tables are, and the subsequent sound waves.

As prediction and actual measurement match ever closer, the load of the system gradually decreases. If the model is right, Na-Yeli might be able to run a second tracking/anticipating program on a second core.

Ideally, the predictive calculations and the data from their Soundcloud should match. Yet it never fully does. Their merging stops at about a 98% match. This is strange, as her state-of-the-art, triple-redundant quantum computer should be able to push matching certainty to well over 99.9%, leaving less than 0.1% for chaotic sound and sensor precision.

Yet, a good 2% remains unpredictable. Nothing to worry about, as her Soundcloud and ELM shield can easily deal with that, but strange nonetheless. Is there yet another, much smaller ball bouncing around? For it to get to the same decibel levels, it would have to move much, much faster, while it would encounter quite a bit more friction from the air in this layer. But nothing of the kind has been picked up by her radar, nor by her lidar.

It's more noise than Chaos Theory–to the best of their knowledge–can account for. It's an unpredictable source of sound that should not be there. Yet Na-Yeli and all her instruments can't pinpoint another source of sound, and it must be huge in order to peak at the levels they're looking at. Not something to be easily overlooked. Or otherwise, Chaos Theory needs to be refined. Which is another option, as Na-Yeli cannot find any known natural environment with these extreme sound levels. Like the way General Relativity could only truly be refined when humanity was able to perform direct measurements and experiments on an existing black hole.

An unexpected sound wave passes through the ELM shield. This was not uncommon when they were just getting started, the system being adjusted as the algorithms were being fine-tuned. That it's happening now, after the system is fine-tuned, and updated with the actual main sources of the sound blasts, is worrying.

Na-Yeli checks the status monitors, but they show no anomalies. The triple-redundant quantum stacks are working fine, the ELM shield's health readings are all above 90%, and the Soundcloud of Kittis all report back as fine and functioning, as well.

If it's not her system, then something unexpected might be happening outside, in this Doom Bells soundscape from Hell? She surely hopes not, because that means their understanding of the dynamics of this system is incomplete, which might get them killed.

Another fierce sound blast coming through, rattling her teeth, hurting her eardrums (which are fully enveloped in sound-dampening foam already). And another. This can't go on: she feels pain in her abdomen, hoping nothing is ruptured yet. Her ears beep and her belly hurts, and she doesn't really want to know what other damage is being done.

She adapts her original program. First, she extends the reach of her Kittis, so they can hear strange peaks sooner. Then she maximizes the reaction time of her ELM shield, which was set a bit lower to save energy. In places like this, she's constantly balancing budgets, feeling like a juggler that's keeping up ever more clubs every time, dreading the moment she can't keep them all in the air. Now, her system is faster while consuming more energy. First, survive this, then see if they've got enough battery capacity left to make it to the South Pole's Diaphragm Gate.

Her tweaks work, as the sound blasts coming through reduce in power and frequency. The disturbances keep going for another two minutes, then–as sudden as they appeared–stop. Na-Yeli lets out a sigh of relief she didn't know she was holding. If things stay calm for the next few minutes, she might set everything back to its original parameters. Or maybe not. Right now she's just glad to be alive.

Things remain, well, not exactly calm, but predictable. They're making good progress, and while Na-Yeli wonders if the 2% of unpredictable noise has something to do with the previous disturbances, and is something her system can handle. In any case, the sooner they are out of this excessively hostile place, the better. But something keeps nagging at Na-Yeli. Her subconscious–which has a direct link to LateralSys–keeps badgering her while she can't quite put her finger on what is off about it. Before she can think about it further, her cameras pick up a flashing light source.

Short/short–long–short/short. The interstellar code for distress (on Earth this used to be S.O.S. in Morse code as short/short/short–long/long/long–short/short/short). Impelled by treaties and ingrained behavior across the galaxy, Na-Yeli has no choice but to check this out, and offer help, if possible.

Luckily, it's not that far from her course, and while her energy balance is slightly negative–she's using more power than she generates–the sound power harvesting parts of her ELM shield greatly extend her battery life. She could do an extra round in this layer if she felt like it. Well, her teenage self liked the odd blast of extreme noise metal, but she knows when she's been outclassed. Anyway, towards the source of the distress call.

Like her own, the outer skin she finds has been aerodynamically shaped for flight, and indeed it does fly, probably because it carries much less weight than Na-Yeli. The alien exoskin is ruptured everywhere, yet the whole delta wing structure has more or less remained in one piece. Na-Yeli matches course and aims her floodlight at the fractured vessel. As far as she can see, the alien spacecraft is empty. She circles it several times, studying it from as many angles as is feasible, but no signs of life.

Somehow, though, parts of the autonomous systems are still running, a testament to their sturdiness (and their designers). The alien craft is using the same type of power harvesting from the Enigmatic Object's fast-rotating electromagnetic field, embedded in its wings, and apparently still connected to its emergency lights, that keep sending their distress message to a stupendously noisy, yet otherwise empty world. Empty of life–current observers exempted–that is.

A lasered siren song in a screaming sky, both extremely sad yet uncannily poetic. After recording it all, there's not much more Na-Yeli can do, apart from putting out the distress signal. But she thinks better of that, as it somehow belongs here, by now.

A monument of endurance in a layer that constantly out-screams itself.

Still, it makes her wonder. Is this environment truly lifeless? What is excessively hostile to some species, might be exactly the right environment for others. On Earth, certain bacteria thrive near deep-sea volcanic vents, at pressures and temperatures that would kill all other Gaian life. There are beings –both alien and human, both natural and genetically modified–who survive and even thrive in the vacuum of space (as long as there's an energy source relatively nearby). Sundiver probes in other solar systems have found signs of plasma beings in the solar corona. So how far-fetched would the existence of beings made from pure sound be?

Na-Yeli doesn't know, cannot possibly know. The 2% they can't explain might as well be some new kind of sonic chaos that is unknown to man. It might be self-sustaining sound sculptures randomly repeating, self-amplifying auditory patterns, an emergent type of übernoise. The chances of it being, by any definition, alive, are exceedingly small. The chances of it being, in any meaning of the word, sentient, are even more insignificant.

But extremely insignificant does not equal zero. And anything above zero is–when it comes to the possibility of life–not negligible. Then there was this episode where her ELM shield let significant sound peaks through: either this was the 2% that fell beyond Chaos Theory's calculations passing through them, or–she knows this sounds crazy–the prodding of curious creatures that see something new, something strange? So if this one-in-a-million chance–better make that one-in-a-kazillion–is true, then they're looking at life. At living beings. She should at least make some kind of record of it, even if it means they need to stay a little bit longer in this cacophonous hellscape.

Suppressing the anxiety that's constantly fueled in this brassy inferno, Na-Yeli forces herself to look at this extremely unlikely phenomenon in the long run. *Something must be sweeping these huge bronze balls along,* she figures, *otherwise, both friction and the energy releases that each extreme sound blast present should have stopped them in their tracks ages ago.* She can't be sure of exactly what keeps powering this ghastly pandemonium, but has a strong inkling, like a quickly rotating neutron star– or black hole–right in the center of this Enigmatic Object. The gravity throughout the layers has to come from somewhere, and apparently, the barriers between the layers do not–or cannot–filter out gravity. When–make that if–she's got time, she might be able to calculate if the frame drag from such a rotating point mass would be sufficient to overcome the air friction and energy losses through bouncing that the oversized, globular Doom Bell surely must suffer.

On top of that, the fast-rotating electromagnetic field might generate currents inside the conductive bronze spheres, which might help push them along, as well. Quite possibly, the speed at which they're moving is the equilibrium between the frame drag and electromagnetic push on one side, and the air friction and bounces against the impenetrable barriers on the other side.

And there's another thing each Doom Bell should be losing–mass. Her probes already measured very high concentrations of metal particles, meaning that each Doom Bell must be losing minute pieces of it at every boisterous rebound. On top of that, it's already quite hot– close to 32 ℃–and since there is no heat sink that she's aware of–and she suspects that the barriers between the layers are near-perfect insulators, otherwise the whole Enigmatic Object would have cooled down to the cosmic background temperature long ago–so over time, it will only get hotter.

Simply meaning that the current situation– never mind how it got into that state–is not going to last forever. Either the mass of the Doom Bells will be low enough so that their bounces will generate lower sound levels, or it will get so hot in here that they will simply melt.

Either scenario means doom for any living beings of pure sound that need this crazy meganoise environment to live, possibly to thrive. *But,* the cynic in her says, *there have been plenty of species both in Earth's history and on many other worlds that have been living on borrowed time as their environment changes while they did not.* Extinction is part of evolution.

No, the compassionate scientist in her says, *a life-form so rare, so quintessentially unique surely deserves its own zoo.* So how can she save them? She can't recreate their environment, so the only thing she can do is copy it, or better, make a computer simulation of it. That should be easy, as her computers now know exactly how this layer works. Also, plenty of processor space is available now as they, seemingly, have the situation under control. If worse comes to worst, and she needs the spare CPU power to survive, she could kill the simulation, but would only do that with a heavy heart.

This will take some time, so she takes a small detour while she sets up the Doom Bells simulation. In the meantime, she tries to analyze the 'two unpredictable percent' as much as possible, looking for recurring processes to the best of her— and the quantum computer's–ability. When the

Doom Bells simulation is up and running, she runs it at a highly accelerated rate, to see if a similar kind of unpredictable noise-within-the-noise arises. After the equivalent of ten thousand years of real-time, the amount of unpredictable noise reaches the 1% threshold.

This encourages Na-Yeli because if nothing showed up in the simulation, it would mean the simulation is too far removed from the real thing, and the copies of the 'real 2%' would probably not survive. Now she hopes they have a fighting chance.

But she also needs to consider if she's not inadvertently creating simulated noise life, which might compete with the noise life she's—even if indirectly—trying to conserve. Throwing some imaginary dice in her mind, she decides to copy the 'real 2%' as much as possible when the 'simulated unpredictable noise' has reached 1.5% in her simulation. This will increase the whole to 3.5%, but she thinks there is plenty of space for the extra 2%.

When that point is reached, she slows the simulation down to real-time and copies the real 2% into her simulation. The whole process takes up about 20% of her third backup computer, a sacrifice she's more than willing to take if it means conserving, no matter how indirectly, what might be a once-in-a-lifetime look at a bizarre new form of life.

Even if it means that the originals will eventually die, their copies—and their copy's descendants—may live on. And be studied. And who knows, maybe someone—thankfully she's not looking at a mirror—would be crazy enough to recreate their original environment, and try to resurrect the originals. *With replaceable Doom Bells, air filtering, and temperature control,* she surreptitiously thinks (and hopes).

She decides to make one final detour through this hyper-level sound layer—all systems are still fine, including back-ups—to see how the simulation develops. The 3.5% unpredictable noise remains quite stable, and she can still recognize reoccurring patterns in the simulation that match the real ones. Now she can only pray to the single god she believes in—most scientists and engineers call them Murphy—begging them to leave her sound beings alone.

Now, she must travel onwards, as the last opening awaits. She hates leaving a layer without discovering its most important secrets, without figuring out what makes it tick. But she should stay here as shortly as possible, to minimize the wear and tear on both her ELM shield and her probes, as she might need them on the way back. And the bow wave of anti-sound her system's producing might actually hurt the–admittedly possible–life in this sonic madness. She was already taking a bigger risk than warranted. *But it's worth it,* her conscience says.

So they arrive at the South Pole's Diaphragm Gate, where Na-Yeli needs to proceed with at least the same caution as with which she entered this penultimate layer, this realm of the Doom Bells. Hovering over the final opening–through the Moiety Alien's floatation powers assisted by the careful flapping of Na-Yeli's exowings keeping her in a figure-of-eight holding pattern–she prepares to send a few probes through. Probes she can now miss, as they've only half a globe to monitor, and her radar will detect the eventual incoming of a massive Doom Bell well in advance.

TOO STRANGE TO LET

As is her wont, Na-Yeli explores the next layer with a few Kittis. They find nothing. No atmosphere in the penultimate layer, just a vacuum. Na-Yeli figured that would happen eventually, in the Core at the least. She does have a high-efficient ion thruster, but its power reserves are–necessarily–limited. The gravitational force of about 1.1 G in this layer will keep dragging her down, and she will not have an atmosphere to fly through–read: to push off against–and possibly no ground to stand on.

Which means that in the Core–if or when she gets there–she needs to achieve an orbit around the extremely massive object right at its center (if her guess is correct). If there is no ground floor to speak of in the penultimate layer–unlike the Fractal Maze, the Sea of Hyperwaves, and the Berserker

Forest–then standing on the inner barrier is no alternative either. Matter-eating spaghettification will take care of that.

She prefers to keep the power reserve of her ion thruster as close to maximum as possible, as she never knows how much she might need it at the core. So she can either enter the penultimate layer and quickly boost herself into orbit, or she can select a slingshot trajectory that moves as close to the inner barrier as feasible. The latter is faster, but also requires much more energy in case she needs to change direction, and dog knows what she–and the Moiety Alien–will run into this time.

Then she gets an inspiration: she can improvise some extra boost, using the materials in the Doom Bell layer. She programs her nanobots to produce a makeshift compressor–driven by a sound-powered generator, similar ones have recharged all her systems–and an air bottle with a nozzle. Her exoskin has been able to extract quite some metal particles from the Doom Bell layer's atmosphere. After a while, she has a pressurized air bottle with a nozzle she can use for course changes as she orbits through the vacuum of the penultimate layer.

What both baffles and worries her is that her probes register almost nothing, just a vacuum with a background temperature of about 40 $^{\circ}$K–about ten times space normal–and nothing else. No strange objects, no light or other sources of electromagnetic radiation, or radiation of any kind that they can measure. Even her Casimir plates measure a normal vacuum. Her instruments are too small to measure either neutrinos or gravity waves –even if she suspects there are plenty of the latter– but neither are a danger to her or her companion.

One of her theories is that all these layers are a test, a kind of filter. Intelligent beings that successfully pass through all of them will arrive at the core to pick up or see something there. A message, a reward, a revelation, *something*. Passing through an empty vacuum is not much of a test, as everybody had already done that just to get to this Enigmatic Object anyway.

So something must be wrong, horribly, undeniably wrong. But what? She can't keep pondering this right here in the sonic madness of the Doom Bell layer forever, as her energy reserves are slowly, yet inevitably depleted. She has to go to the next layer. But she knows so damn little …

She decides to send in one last swarm of Kittis, programming them to make a thirty-minute round trip at full speed, which should take them through, which should take them through most of the southern hemisphere–well hemi-shell would be more appropriate–of the penultimate layer. This lack of information scares her more than anything else.

While the probes make their tour, she thinks about what if. What if she encounters something so crazy, so dangerous she needs extra thinking time? Running constant figure-eight patterns, which means changing orbits every once-and-a-while, takes energy, of which she only has a limited amount. On top of that, here at the South Pole, the electromagnetic field is weakest, meaning precious little recharging abilities.

She scrambles to think of the best energy-saving holding pattern there is, and inspiration strikes. A pogo stick with sacrificial material at its very bottom, so she can jump on and off the inner barrier. She could even use it to jump around that whole layer, if necessary, as the inner diameter is only 14.75 kilometers (as measured by her Kittis). Three hours jumping, four tops.

She has to compactify most of the material of their ELM-shield anyway—as it seems there is no spare material in the penultimate layer—so she might as well partly refurbish some of it into a pogo stick. Even if she may not need it, it makes her feel better.

Most of the probes come back, a few don't. Those that have returned report a frantically rippling magnetic field in the equatorial region and some fast-moving heat signatures. And they confirm the local background radiation of about 40 ^oK, or–in other words–something is heating this layer up. But slowly, very slowly. Something is happening in the equatorial region, and she doesn't trust it. Not one bit.

She has two options. One is diving into the penultimate layer and converting part of the gravitational energy into getting her into orbit– basically around the point mass that she's fairly sure must be in the Core–and once in orbit, her energy expenditure is zero. Disadvantage, she'll be moving fast. If her estimate of the point mass in the Core is correct–about 4.68×10^{19} kilograms, or about twice the mass of 16 Psyche, one of the larger asteroids in Earth's solar system's Asteroid Belt– then an orbit of about 17 kilometers will take her 124 seconds (just over two minutes), traveling at a staggering 1540 kilometers per hour. In other words, only about half a minute before she heads straight into whatever it is at the equatorial region. At fifteen-hundred-and-forty clicks, not much time for–costly–course corrections.

Her second option is to let herself drop down to the inner barrier of the penultimate layer–needing to brake with the makeshift compressed air bottle– and then bounce around on her tailor-made pogo stick until either she's figured out what the hell is happening in there, or the sacrificial material at the bottom of her stick is used up. She wishes she could just hover like the Moiety Alien–she even doesn't understand how it does it, both in an atmosphere and in a vacuum–but it's one of those things she likes to get to the bottom of when they get out of here alive. *If* they get out of here at all.

She can't stay in this blaring pandemonium indefinitely–and she's only got ELM-Shield layers left, so no redundancy–even if it truly is the devil she *knows*. She gestures for the patiently waiting Moiety Alien to follow her and they jump through, one by one. Gravity is stronger in here, slightly more than Earth normal, meaning she needs to expend more energy to break her fall. She points the nozzle of the pressurized air bottle downwards and gently lets out air. She opens the nozzle further until she falls at an acceptable speed, while her radar, sonar, and lidar measure the distance to the bottom.

Different from all previous layers, this penultimate layer is only 2.5 kilometers thick. On the one hand, this will greatly reduce the amount of energy she needs to slow her descent. On the other hand, it makes this seemingly empty layer feel rather claustrophobic in comparison. She still has air left when she finishes her descent, and while the gravity has increased to 1.4G at the inner barrier, she's designed her pogo stick for well over 2G.

During her descent, her instruments try to take in as much information as possible. As far as they can measure, everything from the polar region to the very beginning of the equatorial region is empty, nothing but vacuum between two impenetrable barriers. In the equatorial region, though ...

It's unmistakable on her radar, sonar, and lidar, six giant spheres rolling–or sliding–exactly over the equator. Their diameters match the thickness of the layer, two-and-half kilometers across. They make the sixty-five-meter-across, one-thousand-ton Doom Bells seem tiny in comparison. On top of that, they move faster. Much faster.

They bang against each other all the time at speeds that put a deep, existential fear into her. The speeds her radar, sonar and lidar measure vary from one hundred up to three hundred meters per second. In other units, three-hundred-and-sixty up to well over a thousand kilometers per hour. These humongous monsters sometimes exceed jetliner speeds.

It doesn't make sense. If these giant spheres are solid metal their weight would be about 5×10^{14} kilograms or 500 trillion tons. Ten thousand times as light as the point mass in the Core, but massive enough that she should feel a gravitational pull nearby. But then getting to move at these speeds would have taken a truly tremendous amount of energy. Her estimations showed that the average speed of the Doom Bells–about 40 kph–more or less matched the equilibrium it would have from the energy it gained through frame drag plus the electromagnetic push and the energy it lost through air friction and the über-noisy bounces.

On the other hand, there is no air friction in here. But can frame drag alone accelerate such massive monsters to such monstrous speeds? She somehow doubts it.

On top of that, why do these monsters stay put exactly on the equator? If their diameter fits inside the thickness of this layer, they should be moving all through it. Na-Yeli thanks Murphy that this is not the case, but she would feel much better if she knew why. Dancing on her pogo stick, she increases the measurements of her radar, sonar, and lidar to the highest precision available, and cross-checks all data. There it is–the outer barrier (and the inner one) are not exactly spherical. They have a very slight bulge at the equator and are very slightly flat at the poles. When she compares the measurement of all the six giant spheres–not easy to do at the speeds and bounces they're making, but a statistic average will have to do—it appears that these just exactly fit in the, very minor, bulge at the equator.

While this fact saves her ass, Na-Yeli is baffled. The barriers between the layers—whatever they are —seem impenetrable and cause spaghettification of every solid material that touches them. She's experienced that—actually the bottom of her pogo stick is experiencing it with every languid bounce she makes—up and close, personally. Several times already.

So as these giant spheres roll against the barriers, they should experience spaghettification of their material to its atomic constituents. The massive amount of metal particles in the Doom Bell layer showed that this process was ongoing with the Doom Bells, meaning they were probably much bigger to begin with. So these giant spheres should already have worn down sufficiently so that they would roam all across this layer. Yet they don't.

The Enigmatic Object is old. So either some immensely advanced aliens set up this nightmare trap just before the Moiety Alien and she arrived here—unlikely in the extreme—or this has been going on for quite some time, meaning these giant spheres don't wear down. Meaning they cannot be normal matter, they have to be made from something much, much stronger.

She racks her brain and her database. Neutronium? No, they're way too big to be neutron stars. They would have collapsed into black holes well before they even got close to this size. What if they're hollow? But then they should have collapsed under their own weight, and before that thin slivers of neutronium will experience beta decay, in which case they would have decayed into protons, electrons, and a stupendous amount of freed up energy in the form of gamma rays.

A quark-gluon plasma? That's so hot she'd be burnt to a cinder. Black holes? At that size, they would have merged and swallowed up the whole Enigmatic Object, easily, before you could say 'singularity'.

The only thing left is strange matter or strangelets. Then again, strange stars of that size would also have collapsed into a black hole due to gravitational pressure. So a hollow strangelet? Theoretically, if its surface tension is above a certain threshold, a strangelet could be stable. Still, a hollow sphere of strangelet should implode on itself due to the same gravitational forces. Something must keep it from collapsing.

Maybe they're stuffed? But even the strongest common material–Osmium? Titanium?–would be too weak to resist such pressure. She double-checks her database. Theoretically, strangelets can have a charge, if only for about a few femtometers thick, basically one or two layers of strangelet (a strangelet; that is, an up, down and strange quark, is about two femtometers across). Suppose the inside strangelet layer of this hollow strangelet sphere is charged? And then inside this hollow strangelet sphere, there is a core—which can be normal materials, say ions—that has the same charge, meaning the electromagnetic force keeps the hollow strangelets from collapsing under their own weight?

Madness, but it's the only plausible explanation she can come up with. She has to know, so she sends in a sacrificial probe to measure the magnetic field of one such giant sphere, let it bounce off one of them if necessary. She is indeed already measuring a faint magnetic field, and if she can overcome her fear and gently move closer to the equator with her pogo stick, she should see the intensity of this field increase.

Hop by hop, she gets closer, ready to rocket herself away with the air pressurized bottle, or her ion thruster if necessary, buttocks pinched with sheer anxiety. Bit by bit, the intensity of the magnetic field increases, as well. Extrapolating, Na-Yeli calculates that it should be very strong on the surface of the—she mentally named them already—stuffed strangelets.

The probe returns, and it measured a very strong magnetic field, about 3.2 Tesla, at the very surface it bounced back from—and miraculously came back in one piece. It also shows that there is a liquid sticking to the giant sphere, that is 'shaken off' at every bounce, but immediately after that flings back to the nearest sphere, as if something is attracting it towards them. It even managed to capture a tiny globule of the liquid—Na-Yeli now sees it bounced off several times from the giant sphere as if it had a thrill ride—which Na-Yeli's spectrometer now analyses. Hg and Hg^{2+}. Mercury and Mercury ions positively charged quicksilver where the ions form about 0.6% of the total.

Normally, if she can foresee where two of these giant balls clash against each other, she could easily fly through the spaces between them either near the inner or the outer barrier. Tens, maybe even hundreds of meters of room. Just a matter of careful timing.

But the Mercury changes everything. Positively charged, it sticks to the stuffed strangelets, meaning these are negatively charged. So they must be hollow, with a core of negatively charged ions inside that keep the—also negatively charged—strangelet shell from collapsing under its own weight. The Hg^{2+} ionic Mercury then sticks to the giant stuffed strangelets, and tends to go to where it feels the most negative charge; that is, near the equators of the giant strangelet spheres.

Every time the strangelet spheres bash against each other, the Mercury is shaken off at a tremendous speed, also varying from 100 to 300 meters per second or some seven hundred kilometers per hour on average.

So if Na-Yeli dives through one of the open spaces between the spheres there will be Mercury sloshing at her, Mercury with a density thirteen times that of water moving at the speed of a jet airliner. Quicksilver, indeed. That's not survivable.

Of course, the movement of the Mercury is even more chaotic than that of the strangelet spheres. There is a minor change that she might be missed by it altogether, but that chance is truly unpredictable.

Then her best bet is to dive straight between the middle of two giant spheres right when they part and be through before one of them returns– normally one will meet a neighbor sooner, and bounce back first. No quicksilver in between, as that bounces off to the sides. But if she times wrongly, she'll be squashed flatter than a bug on the windshield of a speeding car, flatter than a probe slamming into a neutron star.

She is committed, she could get back into the Doom Bells layer if she unpacked her compactified

ELM shield, but she's been sent in to complete this mission. Yet she's scared shitless.

She carefully pogos closer to the incomprehensible violence of the equatorial region of this penultimate layer, but the closer she gets, the more terrified she becomes.

Despite her fear, she's already programming her computer systems to take snapshots of the strangelet spheres' positions and momenta, and while the behavior, in the long run, will be chaotic, it should be predictable within certain safety margins in the short run. Like the weather, very good to predict for the next few hours, more difficult for the next few days, and almost impossible for the next few weeks. She's a trained scientist, and it's science, stupid! Just trust the equipment and the calculations, and you'll be fine.

But still, she's deadly afraid. Science doesn't *feel*, doesn't *experience* these unstoppable mountains, doesn't imagine how truly implacable and horribly destructive they are. She's never been so afraid in her life, an existential terror intensified by each soundless mega-bounce, a bottomless dread deepened with each invisible ultra-clash. Something she can't overcome: some people have incurable vertigo, some people have untreatable claustrophobia, she has this. No test ever showed this very singular phobia, how could it? This situation is as unique as the phobia it engenders within her. She's paralyzed with angst so immense it defies description.

And now the Moiety Alien gestures for her to follow it. She waves a definite no-no, bouncing on her pogo stick, whose bottom sacrificial material is slowly running out. The Moiety Alien makes a shrugging gesture–it learned really well–and moves to the violently bouncing giant spheres nevertheless. It accelerates as it approaches them, zigs and zags a bit as it chooses its final trajectory, and then simply dives in. Na-Yeli quickly launches a probe with a powerful torch after it, and even then she has to superimpose the radar/sonar/lidar data to see what actually happens.

It takes all of Na-Yeli's willpower not to close her eyes in abject fear. Time seems to slow down as she watches her companion dive straight into that hyper-kinetic turmoil, seemingly to meet its untimely death as it shoots almost straight into a strangelet sphere, only to see a hole opening, maybe just in time. But no, it closes while the Moiety Alien is diving through, it'll be smashed into a million little pieces ...

But no. Lightning-fast, it squeezes its forward globules, well, forward, as its aft globules, which are near the inevitable collision, shrink to their minimum size. *It won't work*, Na-Yeli thinks at adrenalin hyperspeed, *you can't squeeze them to sub-Planck size*. Then the giant spheres part, and she sees the Moiety Alien move onwards, seemingly unharmed. Only then does she realize that it didn't go straight through the center–where the giant spheres meet–but just a bit off it. A spot narrow enough for it to squeeze through, and where the quicksilver is sloshed aside.

Very smart, she thinks, thankful her companion is still in one piece, *but I can't squeeze myself together like that.*

To make its point, it comes back again two minutes later, beckoning her again, almost impatient, as if saying, *c'mon, it's cool, a piece of cake*. But Na-Yeli has made too many calculations, she knows the masses and the forces involved. They're almost off the scale, and invisible without instruments. Her most powerful torch can only light an insignificant spot on a twenty-five-hundred-meter diameter sphere. Uncontrollable forces operating in total silence and in utter darkness. She can't unsee or unthink them, and the fact that they're both absolutely quiet and completely invisible only adds to her existential terror.

For the life of her, she can't do this. For the life of her, she must do this. Bouncing gently on a pogo stick in a dark vacuum, she's frozen with indecision and fear. Then the sensors at the bottom of her pogo stick tell her that her sacrificial material is running out, spaghettifying into a thin vacuum. She has to act now, but she can't overcome her fear. She faints, probably preferring slow spaghettification above jumping out of existence in the blink of an eye ...

But not KillBitch. KillBitch will never die without a fight, and will always part in a blaze of glory rather than sizzle out right before the final opening. She quickly opens the nozzle of the air pressurized bottle and rises to the diametrical middle of this penultimate layer, following the cues of the 'dive-through' program the Slow CEO did set up but was too frozen in fear to follow up on. Once the bottle is empty, she uses the ion thruster to get her into the correct orbit, then takes the longest way to the other side, in order to come as close as to the orbital speed–almost 800 kph–as possible.

After somewhat more than a third of a turn, KillBitch is meeting the clash of the strangelet spheres head-on. That she's moving with approximately the same speed as the fast-moving, massively bouncing monsters makes her feel good. It gives her a sense of equality, of being at the same level, no matter how false that equivalence, in reality, is.

It's all or nothing, or as digital as an analog life can get. Her body is soaked with adrenalin, her senses operate at top speed and subjective time slows down. KillBitch isn't crazy, as she's following the program's cues. The short-time predictability of these giant, rebounding balls should be good, actually quite easy for the massive computing power of her triple-redundant quantum CPUs. At some point, you just have to trust the program and your own speed and agility.

As she enters the danger zone–the juggling game of the gods–time, for her, slows down to a crawl. The gargantuan strangelet spheres seem to move in slow motion, like globular mountains creeping in a lucid dream. Initially, her course seems to be aimed straight at one, but as she gets closer, as if by magic it moves away.

Slowly, deceptively slowly as the adrenalin in KillBitch's system reaches new record levels. It's as if her soul is alight with holy fire. A gap between two mountainous spheres opens, and as she dives into it, deeper and deeper and deeper, she experiences–through her lidar's reflections–just how huge these stuffed strangelets are.

Then–out of nowhere–she sees something that shouldn't be there. An artifact on a giant artifact (even KillBitch doesn't doubt that the strangelet balls are constructs) that emits radiation of a very specific frequency, glowing in such a narrow spectrum that her spectrometers could not ignore this extremely particular spike. The actual glow is well outside the visible spectrum, so is superposed on KillBitch's vision with false color, in this case, a deep amber. A rapid burst of lidar flashes catch it in 'real'—read: visible to humans—colors and estimates its size as about two meters and its shape as a cylinder, probably a hollow cylinder. Then—in the blink of a hyperactive eye—they're past it.

In the meantime, the gap has reached its maximum size and is narrowing again, while KillBitch sees that she's not yet at the right side of the curve. The slope is still going up, ever so slightly. Then there's no more slope, a piece that's almost straight while the other sphere—also a near-flat surface from her vantage point—is closing in. Like a bug between two rapidly closing hands, like a piece of red hot metal between the hammer and the anvil ...

But she's a quick bug, a damned fast bug. She's a speeding, hot rod, goddamn screeching metal motherfucker. Her face stretched in an all-or-nothing grin, she gets out of harm's way just in time.

Through!

She raises a lone fist to the uncaring forces of destruction, in defiance, in victory. Open wide the dopamine gates, her hormonal system says and she gets the high of all highs, a furious spit in the face of death. For the shortest of moments, she even gets overconfident. *I could turn around and do this again, right now.* But as she moves past the northernmost position of the giant strangelet balls, she sees the Moiety Alien speeding up in parallel of her, about one strangelet ball diameter away. *Since you're here, as well,* KillBitch rationalizes her urge to do it again away, *we might as well stay, and get to the very bottom of this.*

They gradually match their courses inwards, towards the final Diaphragm Gate at the North Pole. As it is, KillBitch just wants to jump through, at full throttle, and get all this shit over with. But somewhere down, deep inside, she knows that's probably not the wisest course of action. So she attaches a fresh layer of sacrificial material on the pogo stick, lowers herself down near the opening, and settles into a gentle bouncing rhythm–the program can, by now, do it automatically with ease –and let the boss take over, again. The chickenshit coward!

BREACHING THE CORE

Strangely, the Slow CEO almost approves of KillBitch's notion of just jumping through. There's nothing to get for them in this penultimate layer, and staying there will just waste energy. So going through and hoping there will be ways to recharge her batteries and resupply her metamaterials is probably right. Of course, behind this Diaphragm Gate could also be another layer of 'just' two point five kilometers thick, and four more. But somehow Na-Yeli thinks that's not going to happen, especially regarding the gravity–at 2.5 kilometers it would become a crippling 50 G.

But–as is her wont–circumspection gets the better of her and she decides that a quick peek-a-boo before going in is prudent. Nevertheless, Na-Yeli's willing to bet good money that there's both a vacuum and a point mass–a neutron star or a black hole–in the Core, anyway. She sends a series of

Kittis, variously programmed to return after five, ten, and fifteen minutes, through the last semi-permeable membrane.

In the meantime, the Moiety Alien does its peek-a-boo routine, shrinking four of its orbitals to minimum size, pushing them through the gate's diaphragm, then blowing them up. Quite far, as Na-Yeli observes, the orbitals on her side shrink to almost minimum size. Then they become their, for what it's worth, 'normal' size and the Moiety Alien pulls its four other orbitals back into the stuffed strangelet layer. Then it nods emphatically, the closest thing to a thumbs-up it can give.

Encouraging, but Na-Yeli prefers to await the findings of her probes. They all return undamaged, with the same reports. There's a vacuum inside the Core, light–electromagnetic radiation varying from the infrared to ultraviolet range–a background radiation temperature of 20 $^{\circ}$K, and a gravitational force at the very center that pulls at the probes with approximately 1.5 G. The pictures of the light emanating from the center are both enchanting and strange–she has to see that light show for herself. None of her probes have measured anything directly dangerous–apart from the extreme point mass in the middle of it all–and Na-Yeli gestures for the Moiety Alien to jump through.

As if eager, it immediately complies and Na-Yeli has to scramble to follow in its ghostly wake. At the other side of the Diaphragm Gate, she immediately has to expend a considerable amount of her energy reserves to get herself into an orbit around the point mass. She can't afford a low orbit, as to get out of that will require more energy than she can store, or generate. She doesn't want to scrape the spaghettifying barrier, either, so settles for an orbit with a radius of fourteen-and-a-half kilometers or two-hundred-and-fifty meters free from the forbidding ceiling. Not that the point mass at the very center is any less forbidding.

As she settles into her orbit–which proves to be, to her surprise, quite a choppy ride–Na-Yeli concentrates on her instruments only. The light show she's witnessed after passing through the last rabbit hole is just too mesmerizing, too distracting. Now that her orbit is stable, she can make a mental progress report, and turn her attention to the light fantastic later.

They made it! They're in the Core, and considering all the remnants of previous expeditions she's seen–and she suspects they're but a small sample of the whole–that's no mean feat. But before she takes stock of the situation right here in the Core, she has one loose end to tie up. The artifact KillBitch spotted as she hurled herself–

her other self has ovaries of adamantium–through the strangelet balls.

She studies the pictures and the data that her instruments could take in the, admittedly, very tight time frame. The cylinder is clearly artificial, someone made it. And there are broken pieces sticking out from it, probably meaning it once was attached to something bigger. What it is, is one question. But the bigger mystery is, how does it stay there?

There's no superglue or other adhesive known to man that could keep such an object in place on a strangelet ball. As they bounce against each other, the speed changes from several hundred kph in one direction to several hundred kph in the other. A momentum change that would break off even welded connections (supposing one could weld anything to strangelet, which is, of course, impossible). So what gives?

A piece of neutronium, kept in place by gravity? She runs a few quick calculations, but even that would be thrown off by the immense momentum changes at every bounce. Also a piece of strangelet, an accidental leftover from the initial construction? Na-Yeli doesn't believe it. Whoever made these strangelet balls would never let such a blemish deface such austere perfection. No way.

She can only tick off the most likely candidates: the four basic forces. Gravity, the electromagnetic force, and the weak and strong nuclear forces. She's already crossed off gravity and sees no way how the weak nuclear force could bind this artifact to the strangelet ball's surface. The strong nuclear force would only work if the artifact was also made from strangelet, and she discarded that idea. So only the electromagnetic force remains. This artifact has to be charged.

It has to be charged very considerably. Extremely considerably. And on top of that, remain charged as it comes into contact–even if intermittently and randomly–with the charged Mercury. Indeed, while Na-Yeli can conceive of a few ways to charge something this drastically, she doesn't see how it could *keep* that charge almost indefinitely. It doesn't make sense, a material that doesn't lose its charge.

If her mind had been a clockwork mechanism, there would have been an audible 'click', as suddenly it clicks into place. There is one type of material–which is still purely theoretical–that can, namely monopoles. Monopoles, according to some, exist only in physical dissertations, in theses about physics. A purely theoretical material, as none of the known alien species–including humanity–have discovered any. With the possible single exception of the HarLeGuins. The HarLeGuins–a race discovered by humans in a constellation named after Ursula K. Le Guin, a race who almost committed communal hara-kiri after the shock of First Contact–announced to have discovered 'the true secret of monopoles', but when asked to deliver proof of their claims, they declined, stating that they want to keep the secret to themselves, suggesting they use the monopoles for their inertialess space drives.

No one has been able to get their hands–or alien appendages–on one of these legendary drives. So the artifact her instruments have spotted might possibly be the remnant of this mythical inertialess drive, supposedly a pure monopole. Interesting, but it'll have to wait until Na-Yeli gets back to civilization. She's got a, well, if not actually bigger, most definitely a more massive, fish to fry.

The light show in here. How can she even begin to describe it? Rainbow-colored structures inside a three-dimensional maze of fairy tale luminescence. Circles within circles within circles. Spirals spiraling out of control. Bubbles upon bubbles within bubbles. All with a transparent gloss of the full visible spectrum, like perfectly round soap bubbles in space. Around the area of the singularity–Na-Yeli doesn't think it's a neutron or quark star for a second, it's way too weird for that–the varying lights are both converged and reflected, appearing like a self-similar structure, a refraction of a constantly varying light, a kaleidoscopic bouquet of fractal sunflowers. While it appears to be self-similar, the whole of it is never really the same. While Na-Yeli realizes that her constantly shifting position is probably partly to blame, it doesn't diminish the magic in the slightest.

It's faint; that is, much less bright than daylight on Earth. Yet it is the dimness that gives the Core's light fantastic a ghostly appearance, an ethereal quality. and a transparent frailty that makes it even more mesmerizing. In this case, less is indeed more.

At a whim, she programs her cameras to check the infrared and ultraviolet sides of the human-centered spectrum, as well. They show the same–albeit in false colors–a dazzling array of circles, spirals, and bubbles at every level whose borders display the full range of its respective spectrum. *So aliens who see in infrared or ultraviolet get the same spectacle,* Na-Yeli thinks, *incredible. A rapture that depicts how we see the light.*

Only after she's shifted her orbit to different tilts, does she find the source of the mesmerizing light show. It's emanating from the singularity at the center, a pulsating beam from its south side. This flashing light beam then reflects against the globular barrier and slightly diverges, then its divergent reflections are reflected and diverge, etcetera and so forth until they disperse into the multihued spectacle Na-Yeli and the Moiety Alien were witnessing when they entered.

It can't be just the reflection of these pulsating beams, there must be something else that gives this amazing depth, this undeniable aura to the light show in the Core. Na-Yeli doesn't want to destroy her sense of wonder by checking her database, she has to figure it out for herself. If it's truly a singularity down there, then it must be gravitational lensing. But if it's a true singularity, how can light escape from it? Now she's caught in a paradox.

Looking at the fantastic light show a bit more clearly, less dewy-eyed, she notices that there's a minor imperfection, a tiny break from the perfect symmetry, a minuscule black splotch in the Core's mesmerizing lava lamp. That's a shame, and more than a little bit irritating. What is it?

If all the light emits from the singularity at the Core, then–logically speaking–this black blemish must be from something orbiting it. Na-Yeli sets her radar, lidar, and sonar to their highest resolution and performs a few complete sweeps of the Core—not that hard in a sphere with a twenty-nine-point-five-kilometer diameter.

Typically, the black hole doesn't show—its diameter probably too small to be picked up by her instruments—but there's a dark sphere with a one-meter diameter orbiting it at a mere two hundred and twenty meters.

That it hasn't collapsed into itself under these immense forces is truly a testament to its engineers. But Na-Yeli estimates the chances of anything living in there at zero. The gravitational forces over there are about sixty-five hundred G. The tidal forces alone will rip anything apart. And even if some enormously extreme type of life still survived over there, the energy—per kilogram—required to move it to a higher orbit is more than any propulsion system she can come up with can deliver. With the single exception of matter/antimatter conversion, but so far nobody has been able to work out a stable solution for containing the antimatter. Countless experimental facilities have gone up in an expanding wave of gamma ray radiation trying to achieve just that.

Unfortunately, whoever that was, is toast. These aliens came close, though. As it is, they literally came *too* close. She gives a silent salute to their achievement and then moves on.

Beautiful as it is, and despite the single blemish of another failed expedition, she can't remain enraptured with this unearthly light show forever, even if she's sorely tempted, after all the things she's been through. But duty calls, and she needs to analyze, if not everything, then as much as possible. Now, while the light is fantastic, the gravity doesn't quite feel right, either.

The gravity field does not seem, or feel, constant. According to her best calculations, Na-Yeli expected to settle in an orbit with a period of 98 seconds, moving at 464 m/s or close to 1670 kph, where she would experience a gravitational pull of about 1.5 G. As far as she can tell, the average gravitational pull might be about 50% stronger than on Earth, but it sure feels choppy and turbulent. As if the gravity varies depending on her location in space. But all her positioning equipment, including her radar, sonar, and lidar carefully measuring her position relative to the outer barrier, pin her at 250 meters from it, at every point of her orbit. If she wobbles, then it's barely measurable.

A turbulent ride that shakes her faith in physics. Well, at least a little. Because other observations seem to indicate that she's slowly going insane.

It started with the Moiety Alien. She's sure, as sure as she can be in this weirdest of all places, that there was only one of them. If it had a twin or an army of clones, then it sure knew how to hide them. So, to the very best of her—normally sharp—observations, they arrived with the two of them: one Na-Yeli (even if with an induced multiple-personality disorder) and one Moiety Alien.

But as she looks at the Moiety Alien, she sees ghostly copies of it—she looks again—before and after it. In the places where it's been, and in the places where it's going to be. At least she hopes orbital mechanics still work.

And it can't be her eyes, as she's seeing it through her external cameras. While these are normally projected straight onto her eyes, she can double-check them on her internal monitors. And on those internal monitors, those ghostly Moiety Aliens appear, as well.

Then something else strikes her. She's been so … distracted, and … enraptured that she never bothered to look straight in front of her, as her radar, sonar, and lidar normally alert her of anything in her path, and her probes didn't report anything like ghostly doubles of themselves, either. She's made quite a few rounds already, and never bumped into anything. Even if her orbit is wobbly, it does always return to where it started. Unsteady, yet stable.

But now she looks in front of her, afraid of what she might see. And there it is, a ghostly image of herself. And one a bit further forward, and more. Each one getting vaguer, more transparent until they fade out of view. And if staring herself in the back isn't awkward enough, what will happen if she looks back ...

She has to, even if she doesn't quite want to. And indeed, ghostly copies of herself in the orbit behind her, all of them also looking back. *If I make it back to the Berserker Forest*, Na-Yeli swears, *I'll teach my megafauna friends to make booze*. Being drunk might equalize this doubled-up double vision. But she knows but all too well that it's not true.

She knows she should focus on the singularity stack in the center of the Core, but these impossible, well-nigh ungraspable phenomena throw her completely off track. A freakish light show is one thing. A turbulent orbit is another. But echoes of herself which—she's now double, well make that triple-checking—do actually seem to exist. Otherwise, her radar, sonar, and lidar are lying, too, even if the echoes they see do get dimmer the farther away they are.

Then she wonders if her radar, sonar, and lidar are reliable, as well. Do they measure actual echoes or echoes of echoes? Or echoes of echoes of echoes? Echoes all the way down? What was this thing called, sanity?

The Moiety Alien doesn't seem to care. It's in a slightly lower orbit than Na-Yeli, a few arc degrees out of the way. Four of its orbitals–Na-Yeli could never tell the eight of them apart, even after they've shrunk and swollen, even after they've changed colors and even mimicked camouflage back in the Berserker Forest–are aimed straight at the singularity, so possibly it's doing something, following its own agenda. Or it's gone past bonkers –which Na-Yeli now sure is–into catatonia.

Now she's afraid that she really has died, smashed to a Planck pulp by the monstrous strangelet spheres, and this is merely a wild dream of the afterlife, LSD visions of the next dimension. All she experiences merely an occurrence at a singularity convergence.

It's getting too much, too overwhelming. Na-Yeli needs to step back, take a breath. She knows it, but is reluctant, as she also knows that there's someone just dying to cast her oblique light as this madness. Once, just this once, Na-Yeli aka the Slow CEO wanted to figure this out completely by herself. Deep within, though, she knows she needs her complete self to find out what the hell is going on. So she swallows her disinclination and lets go, go with the flow, slant as she goes ...

An undetermined time later, the Slow CEO returns to Na-Yeli's conscious fore, together with the anticipated migraine–the price to pay. As the stars and wrinkly white stripes in her vision recede, and the true pain in her frontal lobes rises to the fore, Na-Yeli wishes that this wouldn't be necessary.

But, through a quirk of evolution, or a quality in reality's design, it has to be like this. While humanity tried, it couldn't get all these different qualities seamlessly into one persona. Somehow running the three of them–or even just two–is beyond the brain's capacity, the way running more than one Operating System one computer doesn't work: the moment there are two CPUs–each with its own OS–they become separate computers. Through synthetic biology and genetic modification, humanity tried to make bigger brains, but as the size of the brains increased–helped by artificially accelerated evolution–something else, something ungraspable, something indefinable, some might call it a soul–would get lost. Bigger, faster, but not necessarily better.

Nevertheless, despite–or maybe because of–the price Na-Yeli pays, LateralSys never disappoints. Her sideways self can be arrogant, aloof, and more than a bit bitchy, but she always delivers. On her own, LateralSys might be an autistic genius, an *idiot savant* who compensates her genius by being utterly detached or intensely antisocial, or both. She would not function in a group, let alone a full society of human beings without help—an unfortunate interface, a necessary evil as LateralSys would call it—and forget about communicating with aliens, at all. Like a magpie on acid, the smartest butterfly in the world, she would flutter from glittering enigma to shiny conundrum to ineffable mystery, never caring for the larger picture, unaware of her place in the grand scheme of things. LateralSys will deign to ignore it, but she knows she needs the other parts of Na-Yeli's psyche to survive and to communicate.

In a similar way, KillBitch has certain superior qualities. Her essence stemming from survival instincts honed since time immemorial, she becomes hyper-fast by switching off the majority of the brain's functions—as much as she can get away with without stopping the brain from functioning altogether. Subsequently, both the brain and the body operate at the fastest clock speed possible, with superhumanly fast reflexes. While fear isn't actively suppressed—it's still a major contributor to survival when used right—it's put on lower priority as better alternatives—courage, snapshot decision making, ruthlessness–come to the fore. As with LateralSys, KillBitch comes with a price–an explosive energy expenditure that can only be carried out for a limited time, after which Na-Yeli needs considerable time to recover.

Even the Slow CEO has a price, even if it's not clear up front. While she always tries to find the best possible solution, performing the finest balancing act possible and feasible, the Slow CEO always doubts herself. The moment her decision is made, she has qualms. Even as the solution works as planned–or even beyond expectations–she still has second thoughts, wondering if somewhere in the myriad of possibilities, something even better just slipped through her fingers. This lingering sense of insecurity never really goes away, and–slowly yet inevitably–builds up to a crisis of self belief. While she's not intrinsically suicidal, the Slow CEO needs to be brought back to Earth by her schizophrenic sisters, every once in a while, no matter how much she denies it. It resets her self doubts and immensely increases her feelings of self-worth.

The three of them–together with an ineffable alien, a superposed extraterrestrial infection, and a cast of downloaded beings of pure sound–are now at the center of the greatest enigma of the known Universe. They'll need everything they've got to solve it—or even to figure out a way to solve it—and then get out of here, as well. Secretly, the Slow CEO wishes that LateralSys would invent teleportation, no matter how grisly the details, so that KillBitch could beam the three of them out of here. After they've taken the prize, of course. And to get closer to finding out *if* there is a prize—and if it's indeed there, *what* it is and *how* to get it—Na-Yeli needs LateralSys's report.

> *Paradox, paradox, shining bright*
> *In the Enigmatic Object's darkest night*
> *What lateral mind or eye*
> *Could frame thy supersymmetry?*

I t shouldn't be possible, light escaping from a black hole. Yet the point mass we're orbiting is way too small to be a mini neutron star or strangelet ball, as it's approximately 90 picometers at its largest diameter. Yes, there are ways to measure that with red and blue shifts from carefully targeted lasers. And at that size, and that mass it's most definitely a gravitational singularity.

Theoretically, there is one solution for this: a so-called naked singularity. In technical terms, the solution is a Super Extreme Kerr Object—

SEKO–which is a black hole rotating so fast that its centripetal force overcomes its gravitational force, allowing photons (and other particles) to escape from it. That's because the event horizon has been lifted.

In our Universe, nobody has been able to create a SEKO because the moment you want to accelerate the rotation of your rapidly rotating Kerr black hole to the exact point where rotation overcomes gravity, the particle(s) used to provide that extra rotation somehow get gobbled up by the black hole, increasing its mass just enough so that it remains non-naked. Or, if they come in at the wrong glancing angle, they don't provide enough momentum to push the Kerr object over the edge. Hence the beings who produced this must have a trick up their sleeve that we–and several aliens masterminds– haven't thought of. Or they have a different advantage, which we're not aware of.

Because of the extremely high rotational speed, the mass has become a ring (a flattened torus) and through this ring, messages can be sent. It's now a portal to a different place, most probably to a different Universe.

While light can now escape from this naked singularity, we must also realize that a black hole–except for some faint Hawking radiation and thermal blackbody radiation—is not a source of light. That pulsating light beam—that disperses into the light show that so mesmerizes you through an effect called reverse critical opalescence—must come from somewhere, possibly even from another Universe altogether.

FYI: when matter falls into a rotating black hole, some of it gets sucked in beyond the event horizon, but some of it will rotate around the black hole, forming an accretion disk. The infalling matter, on its way to the event horizon, heats up and sends out radiation (until it disappears beyond the event horizon). If the black hole is big enough, and if sufficient matter falls into it—it's absorbing a sun or planet—then the radiation can be seen over astronomical distances, and that radiation has a certain characteristic called critical opalescence. This is akin to the critical opalescence that some liquids or gasses experience when they go through a phase shift: at first, the liquid (or gas) is clear, then—at the very threshold of the phase shift—cloudy bubbles begin to form until their milky cloudiness completely overrules the liquid's opacity. Critical opalescence turns the phase-shifting liquid (or gas) fully opaque, until the phase shift is completed, after which the gas (or liquid) becomes transparent again.

The critical opalescence of a black hole is actually the accretion disk filtering out the higher frequencies of the radiation of the infalling matter. In other words, the disk luminosity will only have the low-frequency component, as the critical opalescence opaques the higher frequencies. However, with a naked singularity, the radiation–from the infalling matter–*will* feature the high energy (and high frequency) tail.

On top of that, the thermal blackbody radiation of a black hole with a mass larger than that of the Moon will be colder than the cosmic background temperature, meaning that its Hawking radiation–the radiation it's emitting–is less than the radiation it's absorbing from the cosmic background radiation. In other words, such black holes will only gain mass–even if tremendously slowly–and will only start to shed mass if the cosmic background radiation–through the expansion of the Universe–becomes lower than the black hole's blackbody temperature as defined by its Hawking radiation.

However, if the mass of a black hole is lower than that of the Moon, its blackbody temperature as decided by its Hawking radiation is higher than the cosmic background radiation, and it will effectively shed mass–again, at a tremendously slow pace. If my assumptions are correct, then the mass of the naked singularity is about a fifth of that of asteroid Vesta, and a black hole with half the mass of Vega will have a blackbody temperature of 1220 Kelvin. So I'm estimating our naked singularity's temperature at about 2600 Kelvin, or pretty bloody hot.

Since the event horizon is lifted, the black hole's own blackbody radiation does not experience critical opalescence, meaning its higher frequencies are not filtered out. But this is only a tiny amount of radiation—mostly in the infrared—measured in femtoJoules. Hence, the blackbody radiation is not sufficient to power the light effects you see. Therefore, the light is not powered by the naked singularity itself but is sent through it—by someone in the other Universe—and not filtered by critical opalescence.

Presto: the pretty light show you have been—and are—witnessing.

On top of that, this SEKO is highly charged, as you—and everybody else in here—have noticed through the fast-rotating electromagnetic field. This probably also influences the light show in this place, but also provides an easy way for intrepid explorers to recharge their batteries as if somebody really wishes that at least some of us make it to the Core.

Do keep in mind that this particular SEKO has a portal or eye of only about 70 picometers across. This means it's too small for the smallest atom—Hydrogen—to pass through. An atomic nucleus can pass through—like the H^+ ion—and all types of (electromagnetic) radiation. However, there might be areas of negative gravity inside the ring—gravity becomes repulsive through dilatonic effects, which prevents the passage of massive particles—so if you want to send signals through, it's best to use the lightest particles possible, like, you know, massless photons, to make sure they get through.

And the fact that these light beams are pulsed is interesting, to say the least. Unless you believe the aliens who created this Enigmatic Object only put up all these hurdles as a kind of entrance fee before you can witness the weirdest natural light show in the known Universe. Until proven otherwise, we must assume that there's a reason these aliens want us here. If these pulsed beams are their taps on our shoulder, we should consider tapping them back.

However, in a SEKO–and some other black hole solutions–there is another event horizon: the Cauchy horizon. Space and time are mixed here in the Core because both the event horizon and the Cauchy horizon are lifted. The lifting of the–for a lack of a better word–'normal' event horizon means that space-like geodesics sweep from the SEKO, which, together with the now unleashed dilaton field effects cause the wobbles in the gravitational force you experience. While interesting–do record them for posterity–you can ignore them.

The lifting of the Cauchy horizon is another matter, though. Just outside it, closed space-like geodesics exist–the shortest possible lines between two points on a curved surface–which is normal in a large enough gravity well in our Universe, and these are normally contained within the 'normal' event horizon (which usually envelops the Cauchy horizon). Inside the Cauchy horizon, closed time-like geodesics exist –the shortest possible lines between two times– this means if you cross time-like geodesics, you literally travel in time.

If the Cauchy horizon is lifted, as well, then nothing is containing these closed time-like geodesics anymore, meaning they might be everywhere here in the Core. They might be mixed with the usual closed space-like geodesics, and because of frame dragging they might not emanate in concentric circles from the SEKO, but rather be slightly ellipsoid. Which most probably means that we, in our orbit, are crossing closed time-like geodesics at every turn. Thus we are traveling in time. Because we cross the time-like geodesics, we see the future and past echoes of ourselves (and those of the Moiety Alien).

However, the mathematics is extremely complex and not fully clear. So I don't know if we are traveling forward in time, or backward, neither how fast. So don't be surprised if we meet our past selves when–I certainly hope *when*, not *if*–we get out of here. On the other hand, if we are moving forwards in time, we might try to get our business in here done a.s.a.p., because dog knows at what time in the future we might be heading back.

Not to put any pressure on you...;-)

–LateralSys;

Contrary to what her weird systers KillBitch and LateralSys might believe, Na-Yeli the slow CEO thrives on working out solutions under pressure. She might shit her pants when she's between mountains moving at stupendous speeds, she might not come up with ideas so out of the box that the box itself starts to question its own existence, but once a problem not involving mad heroics nor non-existing mathematics is laid out before her, she can move onto it like an unstoppable force.

Zoom out first and ignore little details like time travel, dilatonic effects, Cauchy horizons, and critical opalescence. The big picture is that this is a SEKO, a naked singularity.

For the gravitational effects throughout the Enigmatic Object, the hyper-advanced aliens who made this might also have used a Kerr black hole–one that's only rotating very fast. A SEKO is much harder to produce and maintain, so it must be there for a reason.

If LateralSys is right, then the SEKO is a portal to another place, most probably to another Universe. Suppose that this is the Universe of the hyper-advanced aliens. Normally the two universes are separated from each other, but this SEKO connects them.

It's hidden behind the craziest and most complex labyrinth in our known Universe, so presumably, the other-Universe aliens don't want just anybody–crazy Eddy, mad Suzy, their cats, dogs & neighbors–to be knocking on their doors. Only the very best–the most intelligent and brave–get through.

It makes no sense for the hyper-advanced aliens to constantly transmit a message through the SEKO, as they have no idea–unless they somehow monitor the openings between the layers–if or when some alien of this Universe will come through. *So basically, it's up to me to start knocking,* she finishes her train of thought.

She didn't come unprepared, as there have been communication protocols for this for a very long time. They establish the basic Universal constants–at least for this Universe–and, what we assume is, basic mathematics, using a binary system that can be easily transmitted through pulses and pauses. On top of that, if the equipment from the other side is up to it, amazingly fast transmission rates can be achieved.

So Na-Yeli prepares to send the first protocol the next time–she completes a full orbit every 98 seconds–she faces the north-side opening of the ring singularity, let's call it 'the eye of the SEKO'. She's done some measurements, and the intensity of the light exiting the south-side of the SEKO's ring is in the order of magnitude of the photon density emitted by the Sun at its corona. In comparison, the best laser beam she can send into it will be scattered before it even reaches the SEKO's opening, let alone that anything coherent from her signal can get through. So she must send her signal in at the non-emitting north-side of the naked singularity.

She's repositioned her orbit so that she faces the ring singularity's opening straight-on twice per rotation. Her probes have carefully measured the radiation coming out of its south-side, and they're your ordinary, run-of-the-mill photons, even if packed extremely tight. If all else fails, she wants to capture those—before they reflect and become part of the enchanting light show—to see their original structure. But first, she wants to try to send a message through.

But at which angle? Only when exactly facing the eye of the SEKO? That would limit the usage of this portal quite heavily. Huge masses do bend light, and astronomers are well aware of the effects of gravitational lensing. But this black hole doesn't have that much mass—it's about twice as heavy as 16 Psyche from the Asteroid Belt, or about $1/1700^{th}$ of the mass of the Moon. It will barely bend the path of her photons, so she should be able to send her message in at quite a wide angle. She decides to send the tried-and-true communication protocols in an almost 180-degree arc facing the singularity's ring opening at the north-side, utilizing about 50%

of her orbiting time. On purpose, she selects a relatively low transmission rate, hoping to establish contact first before increasing the frequency of her pulses.

On top of that, her aim has to be true. The dilaton field effects vary the gravity field, making her orbit quite wobbly. And she's aiming at a hole of a mere seventy picometers. However, according to LateralSys, the gravitational lensing effects will help her a little bit, allowing her to be a couple of picometers off. Great help that is, indeed.

She has to assume that part of her message won't get through, so she has to double or triple up the message, insert repetitive pieces with fault corrections. But even that won't help if she misses her goal altogether, and nanometer wobbles are already way too big, and what she feels must certainly be micrometer wobbles, at least.

Just shoot anyway and hope chunks get through? Not a good way to get a message across, let alone a good way to make a first impression. She could try to measure the exact wobbles she makes during the 180-degree arc she tries to send it through, and compensate accordingly. Measure with better than nanometer precision, and then compensate with better than nanometer precision, while incorporating the lightspeed lag over 14.5 kilometers (48 and $1/3$ rd nanoseconds). Nanoquick nanomachines. Unfortunately, they operate too close to the quantum level, so that random chance throws a spanner in the works.

A measly 70 picometer opening. Na-Yeli understands that a larger opening would have required a larger black hole whose gravitational effects would have wreaked havoc through all the layers of this Enigmatic Object. But this quest for precision is inhumane ...

Or she can move into a closer orbit, but this will bring her not only into an immensely massive gravitational field–which will mash her to a very fine pulp–and even if she somehow survived it, she would not have the power to escape that deadly attraction. For her own sake, she's marked the 10-kilometer distance from the SEKO as the safe distance.

Next possibility, move a probe into closer orbit and use it as a relay? But even at one hundred meters from the SEKO, the gravitational field is a distressing three point one million G. Not even her sturdiest–non-Kitti–probes can withstand the tidal forces in that orbit.

Then she wants to slap her head. She was focusing too close, didn't see the forest for the trees. Just aim a wide beam at it, wide enough that she can't miss it. Some 99.99999% or so will miss, but one section–exactly 70 picometers across, plus a few extra picometers thanks to gravitational lensing–will simply beam through.

Easy as pie, and fuck the wobbles. Just make the beam wider than the wobbles, and presto.

Because of this, it takes her several rotations to get the full protocol through–slightly under nine minutes–after which she will wait a similar period, and then try again. But she doesn't have to wait long, as the pulsed beams exiting from the south-side from the eye of the SEKO right after her next 180-degree arc are changing.

Wow, that didn't take long, she thinks, *but let's analyze these first, lest they're not my own signals beamed back at me*. LateralSys's remarks about the closed time-like geodesics and time travel are fresh in her mind. The communication programs quickly assure her that it's not the original signal they sent– not the exact one, neither a mirrored nor otherwise scrambled version of it–but a truly new signal.

That was the good news. The bad news is that they can't make sense of it quite yet.

–some things seem to make sense– the communication AI signals *–while others are opaque. it's almost as if some of their physics are quite similar to ours, while some of it is quintessentially different. we're looking for the best common ground. unfortunately, this might take time–*

Time is not something Na-Yeli wants to waste—especially since she doesn't know if they're inadvertently traveling forward or backward in time—so she decides to test if she can increase bandwidth. "I'm going to resend the protocol, but then with a higher transmission rate," she says, "if we get something back, just quickly tell me if it's exactly the same message—"

—*but then at a higher rate*— the communication AI anticipates —*roger*—

Na-Yeli doubles the transmission rate and waits. In the next arc, she receives an answer that just feels twice as fast. —*same message, double speed, roger*— the communication AI confirms.

She doubles the transmission rate again, gets pinged back, and keeps increasing the messaging ping pong until they reach the maximum transmission rate of her equipment. *Cool*, Na-Yeli thinks, *I can send them the whole Encyclopedia Galactica in about forty seconds. Now if only we could understand what we were sending.* Which is the communication AI's job.

"Made any progress, yet," Na-Yeli asks it, "don't tell me you've been twiddling your quantum thumbs while I increased our communication speed."

—*i?*— The communication AI sounds miffed —*i thought this was a group effort*—

"Never mind," Na-Yeli says, "have you deciphered the message? Time literally doesn't wait in here."

–it's rather strange– the communication AI signals *–the parts where we agree on the physics are crystal clear. then there are parts that//in my best estimation//they talk about completely different physics, and these are completely opaque to me. we might need a physicist who can think outside the box// far outside the box//for that–*

"Not quite yet," Na-Yeli says, the aftermath of the migraine after LateralSys figured out the naked singularity still fresh in her mind, "there's more to life than just physics. How about mathematics, philosophy, and–supposedly your *forté*–language?"

–mathematics is the same story: huge areas of consensus, but similarly large areas where we diverge. i am frantically trying to figure out a language from the areas where we seem to agree, however, to go from basic planck units to explaining that you are a stupefyingly complex organic being evolved on a faraway planet over billions of years, let alone that I am a machine consciousness created by people like you is quite another thing. for that, i need a basic intermediate language before i can even think of getting to something esoteric like philosophy–

"What happened to Babelfish?" Na-Yeli smiles for the first time since they left the Berserker

Forest. If only they had more time. "Don't answer that. First things first, like, we are communicating? Questions and answers, exchange of information?"

–in a way, we are– the communication AI signals *–but only like two alien physics and math professors who try to solve each other's puzzles. i need to establish basic language protocols first–*

"That can take forever and a day, and we simply don't have that long," Na-Yeli says in her strictest managerial tone. "While we are humanity's representatives, we also need to recognize when something is too big for the two–or four, if you wish–of us to handle. We need an army of scientists to analyze their science. We need all the linguists we can get–and I'm sure you'll be one of them–to figure out their language. Right now we have established First Contact, which is great. But we need to follow up with a Second Contact in which our side is better prepared."

–and let all the others take the credit– Sometimes Na-Yeli wonders who programmed the communication AI's faux feelings, as strong AI is only achievable through massively distributed neural networks, much too big to take along on a trip such as this *–we have a unique chance to write history–*

"If we get back in one piece, we've already written history," Na-Yeli says, "right now we must not put the mission in peril by taking on more than we can chew. Knowing the limits of what we can achieve is paramount. Now—and this is a direct order—use all your resources to ask the aliens if they can show us how to set up a naked singularity so that we can contact them after we're out of here, and have all our resources available."

—*that won't be easy, either*— the communication AI signals.

"But much easier than establishing a completely alien language from scratch. Stick to the physics and maths we both agree upon, use some universal representation for sender and receiver, establish them as the former and us as the latter, and get to it." Na-Yeli's voice echoes with the single-mindedness of a thousand CEOs. "On top of that ... "

—*first, my mission is cut short*— the communication AI protests —*and now it's lengthened, again*—

"Ask them if it's possible to temporarily increase the SEKO's charge," Na-Yeli says. "Doubling that will halve our recharging time, and halve our temporal displacement."

—*easy as that*— the communication AI is at a loss.

"While our electromagnetic recharger is working at full throttle, and the field strength is higher this close to the SEKO, it'll take over four hours before it's done," Na-Yeli says. "Hours that may translate into years, or centuries when we get out of this crazy Core. The sooner we're recharged, the better."

–understood– the communication AI signals *– working on it–*

Mere seconds later, the communication AI announces: *–higher SEKO charge initiated when you give the signal–*

"That fast?" Na-Yeli's voice echoes admiration. "I'm impressed."

–i'm not totally useless– the communication signals with a flair for drama *–admittedly, a stupendous fast transmission rate helps, as well–*

Compliment yourself and your manager, Na-Yeli thinks, *who taught it to manage its manager?* Out loud, she says: "Ready for higher SEKO charge in five seconds. Five, four, three, two ... "

–and done– the communication AI signals.

Na-Yeli's instruments record the increased charge the moment it hits, doubling in intensity in a few minutes. *Makes sense*, she thinks, *after establishing contact it's also–supposedly–in the intra-Universal aliens' best interest if we can get out of here. Magically doing away with this whole Enigmatic Object will most probably be physically impossible.*

Even at the maximum possible rate that her recharging cells can handle–and that Na-Yeli has requested, and received–a full recharge of all her batteries will take about two hours. Hopefully, the other thing she requested will get through. While the realization dawns on Na-Yeli that she may not be leaving the Core with the Holy Grail, the Theory of Everything, or any other secrets-cum-treasure of the Universe, she does need to leave with something that proves her story. Irrefutable evidence that she has indeed witnessed a naked singularity–and not dreamed one up–and did have contact with aliens from another Universe.

She wonders if she should already send in probes to check if the layer with the terrible strangelet balls is still the same, or has changed in some unforeseen way. But for the moment she puts it off, as it seems like going a bit too fast. Maybe some unexpected info gets through via the communication AI and she might need those probes for something else altogether. Hopefully, her second request isn't too difficult for the communication AI–and she certainly hopes its pride doesn't stop it from coming back to her if it is too ambitious or just too crazy–nor if it is misunderstood, or turned down by the intra-Universal aliens.

Then she remembers the Moiety Alien. Will it be ready and willing to follow her? It's in a slightly lower orbit that's also slightly tangential from hers.

The Moiety Alien is preceded by a bow wave of its future selves, and followed by a slipstream of its past selves, reminding Na-Yeli that time is both weird and at a premium in here. She's trying to ignore the fading echoes of her time-shifted selves in between which she's sandwiched. And the recording of the light fantastic show is ongoing, thank dog she has more than enough memory space to spare to record as much as possible of it.

As there is no dispersing medium in the vacuum of space inside the Core, she cannot see if the Moiety Alien–and its ghosts–are sending/receiving any beams from the intra-Universal aliens, as well. She suspects–and secretly hopes–it is. While she did save the Moiety Alien back in the layer with the sea of hyperwaves, it reciprocated by helping her, saving her ass more than once in the process, as well. In her book, the Moiety Alien is entitled to its voyage of discovery, as well.

Maybe it finds out something she and her crew don't. Maybe the Na-Yeli team has found something the Moiety Alien hasn't. But from the moment on she helped it, and most definitely when it helped her back, the relationship between them changed from competition to cooperation, and–as far as Na-Yeli is concerned–will remain that way. Call it the Slow CEO's intuition–she imagines KillBitch rolling her eyes at such naïveté and LateralSys wondering why she takes the trouble–or file it under the belief that truly intelligent beings have higher ethics, as well. The huge, cold Universe is hostile enough as it is, humanity–and other aliens–certainly don't need more hostility. Especially not if we–humans and aliens–want to plan for true longevity.

Her wishful musings are interrupted by a ping from the communication AI.

–receiving a message that may, or may not, be the blueprint for a seko that you requested– it signals, *– to be frank, I can't tell–*

"Send to me and let's see if I can make sense of it," Na-Yeli says with more authority in her voice than she truly believes she has in that particular subject. But somebody else might.

Na-Yeli looks through the message and does recognize several formulas involving Planck units and universal constants, but finds other formulas that seem–and a quick database check-and-compare confirms–utterly unknown to her. *This is where it comes to the crunch*, she thinks, *I asked for something truly new, but how do I recognize if it truly is something new, and not some gibberish to throw me off?*

The Slow CEO also knows she has no time to figure it out for herself. Know your limits, she preached to the communication AI and now she must practice what she preaches. Also, they still need well over one hundred minutes to finish a full recharge of their batteries, so she might as well take a short power nap, as she does not know when she gets time to rest, again. Figuratively, she leans back, relaxes, lets go, and waits for LateralSys to take over ...

ven when–possibly, especially when– humans achieve their most ambitious goals, regrets rear their ugly heads ... Na-Yeli reading the commemoration at her father's cremation, the hardest thing she's ever done ... Half their family not showing up because he wasn't buried according to their religion's prescribed rituals ... Oh daddy, why did you die so soon, in that faraway country? ... Why didn't you live to see your daughter finishing her Ph.D., summa cum laude ... Why weren't you there when I was selected as humanity's sole representative ... You would have been so proud ... and I would have melted from pure happiness ... now I'll have to settle with making humanity at large happy ... I still miss you ...

The dream–or was it a memory–fades away and the Slow CEO is back. To her surprise, LateralSys's note is quite concise.

> Wow!
> What you–nay, we–have in here is stuff that will revolutionize physics. I could spend hours, no days, no weeks just double- and triple-checking it and going through all the implications. But we don't have that time.
> To the best of my knowledge and according to my deepest–don't laugh–intuition this feels right. If my intellectual hunch is correct–and I'm willing to bet the farm it is–then this is not only a blueprint for making a naked singularity (which you requested) but has in it the roots to unite Einstein's relativity with quantum mechanics, one of the Holy Grails in physics for long centuries.
> Now let's get the hell out of here before we literally run out of time. But girl, o girl this is the stuff of a once-in-a-lifetime breakthrough. Can't wait to really dig into this, so do get us out of here alive and kicking.
> Well done.
>
> –LateralSys;

A compliment from LateralSys? The Slow CEO thought she'd never see the day. More importantly, though, if LateralSys is that succinct, time is really of the essence.

"About thirty minutes until we're fully recharged," Na-Yeli tells the communication AI, "and then we're out of here. So use your remaining time with the intra-Universal aliens wisely."

–well, they seem to have a request for us– the communication AI signals *–as far as I can understand, they want all the data of our current knowledge about, well, everything. or as much as we carry, and can send–*

"They don't waste time with trivialities, either," Na-Yeli says, "but is this purely as a thank-you for refueling us?"

–they do seem to indicate//again, as far as I can tell//that they will reciprocate– the communication AI signals *–not that we'll have the time to check if they sent us the real thing, or the macguffin to end all macguffins–*

Now it's up to the Slow CEO to make another quick decision. Is it smart to do this? Will it not rob us (humanity) of our bargaining chips if–and when –we make Second Contact? Or is this the move she has to make to be allowed at the very negotiating table? The final test after all the–for lack of a better word–previous tests she went through just getting here?

And does a database–no matter how large–really represent the true creativity and uniqueness of the human race? Knowledge is power, but knowledge is not static, either. For knowledge to remain powerful, it must be developed constantly. And by the time–she hopes–they return, humanity and all the other alien races will have developed more, newer, and hopefully better knowledge.

Na-Yeli has to take a leap of faith. Is she handing them the keys to our Universal Kingdom, unleashing an invasion of unstoppable, ominously powerful aliens? Na-Yeli doesn't think so. If these inter-Universal aliens are powerful enough to set up an Enigmatic Object like this, with impenetrable, spaghettifying barriers, Diaphragm Gates with semi-permeable membranes, and a naked singularity at the very core, then they could probably do much worse. They would have 'invaded' through the eye of a SEKO–a much larger one–already. No, they're staying in their Universe for a reason.

There is something else behind this, but the more she thinks about it, the more it feels like the next step in their mutual approach. *In the end, I was carefully selected to represent humanity*, Na-Yeli thinks, *and to make this kind of decision, wrong or right*.

"Send them the full Encyclopedia Galactica and everything else we know and have handy," she tells the communication AI, "can we send that in, well, under fifteen minutes?"

–at this transmission rate, under ten– the communication AI signals *–are you sure–*

"As sure as I'm going to be," Na-Yeli says, a cleansing kind of serenity washing over her, "do it."

–sending– the communication AI signals.

In the meantime, Na-Yeli launches ten of her Kittis towards the North Pole Diaphragm Gate. If these report no changes from when they left the stuffed strangelets layer, then they can be out of here the moment their batteries are fully charged, and if her companion is ready, as well. She waits–less than a minute–until the Moiety Alien's orbit and hers bring each other close again, and then pings the Moiety Alien with the laser sequence signaling 'are you ready to go?' Right after the sequence hits it, Na-Yeli recognizes the wobbles in its orbitals as 'coming right along'.

–full database sent– the communication AI signals *–receiving a new message–*

Finally, her probes return from their reconnoiter in the stuffed strangelets layer. Instruments measuring a vacuum–no atmosphere to speak of–and a background radiation of 50 °K. No radiation of any kind except the SEKO's fast-rotating electromagnetic field (also twice as strong as before, which makes Na-Yeli wonder if she should ask the intra-Universal aliens to set it back to its previous strength, but she decides against it).

At first sight, they seem alright. But not all of them are. Two of them–from the ten total she sent in–have holes in them, as if something unstoppable passed through them, obliterating all material that happened to be in its way.

–huge file received– the communication AI signals *–about the same size as we sent. first analysis shows a lot of essential differences, though–*

Na-Yeli barely hears it, her full attention on the two damaged Kittis and their reports. *What the hell,* she thinks, *the moment things seem to be going smoothly ...*

–to be concluded in *Forever Thrilled*–

If you liked this novel, please consider leaving a review at:

* Apple Books;
* BookBub;
* Goodreads;
* or on your personal blog;

Every review helps, thank you!

Dedicated to those who wish to go where no-one has gone before. My late father Jan de Vries was one of them.

ABOUT THE AUTHOR

Jetse de Vries has been a commissioning engineer, troubleshooter, trainer, travelling all five continents. He nearly froze to death at Salar de Uyuni, suffered heatstroke in Purnululu, got lost in Ahmednagar, faced elephants in Maamba, and has witnessed ten total solar eclipses. He's trying to settle down as a science fiction writer.

He's had over sixty short stories published, was part of the *Interzone* editorial team and edited **Shine**–an anthology of optimistic SF for Solaris Books. He's blogging about almost anything including consciousness on his substack The Divergent Panorama: https://jetse.substack.com .

Forever Curious is his first novel, part of a duology of which the conclusion called *Forever Thrilled* will be published sometime 2024. A second duology and a trilogy are upcoming.

www.ingramcontent.com/pod-product-compliance
Lightning Source LLC
Chambersburg PA
CBHW051336020726
47501CB00007B/2111